QUESTS
&
ANSWERS

~ A Founder's Anthology ~

With seven original stories by:

H.L. REASBY

GARTH REASBY

QUIANA KIRKLAND

REN CUMMINS

Available books by these authors:

H. L. Reasby

Sekhmet's Light:

Akhet

Peret

Garth Reasby

The Children of Divinity:

Awaken

Ren Cummins

The Chronicles of Aesirium:

Reaper's Return

The Morrow Stone

The City of the Dead

Reaper's Flight

Into the Blink

The Crook and the Blade

The Middle Age: A Geek's Journey from Boy to Man

Volume 1

Published in the United States by Talaria Press, Seattle, WA.

Edited by Quiana Kirkland

Cover by Garth Reasby

Formatting by Ren Cummins

Printed through CreateSpace; First edition: 2012

ISBN-10: 1470024357

ISBN-13: 978-1470024352

Dedications:

For my Gramcracker, who taught me all the good curse words and whose Piglet and Mr. Samuel Whiskers voices cannot be matched by any other grandmothers ever.

~ Quiana

Q to the H to the R: the Gatekeeper, The Trusty Rifle and the Pointman. You made this happen.

~ Garth

For my nephew, Nicolas. Although we haven't seen each other for a very long time, I will always love you and think of you all the time.

~ Heather

To Elizabeth and Jillian, and the rest of my friends and family that knew I could do this; and also for a couple of my high school teachers who were pretty sure I couldn't.

~ Ren

CONTENTS:

QUESTS & ANSWERS

Quests & Answers

Lioness in the Grass

By H. L. Reasby

Author's Note: This story is one that's alluded to in Akhet, the first book of the Sekhmet's Light series. In the book, Nicole finds a series of scrolls detailing the background of the goddess Sekhmet and the stories of several women who bore the title of NuruSekhmet throughout Egyptian history. Lioness in the grass is the story of Kiya, the first woman to ever don the armor.

* * * * *

The gazelles broke cover first. These were the most slender, most graceful, and quickest of the troupe, and they bounded and twirled and danced around and between the gathered nobles so that they barely seemed to touch the ground. Their entrance was greeted by enraptured sighs from the ladies and applause by the men, though their appreciation of the dancers was for very different reasons. As the nobles watched, the gazelles gathered at the fountain in the center of the hall, the horns of their masks dipping as the dancers sank down to drink as though from a watering hole.

Next, the drums started up their martial cadence, heralding the arrival of the lionesses. The remaining dancers slipped from the alcove, moving in lithe half-crouches, and Kiya, who was the leader for this hunt, silently issued commands, using her hands only to simulate the flick or turn of an ear.

The crowd hushed in anticipation and Kiya did her best to ignore the fact that tonight she performed for the son of Horus himself, the Pharaoh. Slowly... slowly... ever so patiently, the lionesses crept forward on all fours toward the "unknowing" gazelles.

Kiya paused suddenly, delighting the younger daughter of a Nomarch, a governor of one of the many provinces that made up the nation, by pausing right beside her cushion. One of the gazelles had raised her head to look around.

Did the prey see her?

Kiya ignored the touch of the girl's hand against her side (this was likely the closest that she would ever come to actually touching one of Sekhmet's sacred lions) and waited for the gazelles to resume drinking. As soon as the dancer lowered her head again, Kiya continued forward, feeling the eyes of the King upon her as keenly has she had felt the noble child's touch.

Kiya paused once more at the edge of the dais elevating the thrones and checked the positions of her fellow lionesses. Tonight would be the finest hunt yet, she told herself with fierce pride as she sprang forward.

The instant Kiya charged, the other lionesses followed suit and the gazelles broke in panic. Two of her lionesses harried after dancers that were not their target, leaping, darting, and twisting to chase without injuring any guests.

The rest remained with Kiya. They quickly boxed in the gazelle, forcing her back to Kiya so she could pounce upon the prey creature. Deft fingers dipped into a fold of the fabric around her hips and retrieved a tiny bird's egg which had been emptied and refilled with red paint. As Kiya dipped her head for the 'kill', she crushed the egg, providing a realistic flow of blood that set the guests into a frenzy of applause... which only intensified when Kiya, following a sudden inspiration, smeared 'blood' on her throat and chest, then sat back on her haunches to roar her victory to the gods.

A hand came to rest on Kiya's shoulder, startling her out of her reverie. As she let the gazelle-dancer get up, she turned and found Ayala crouched close to her.

"You are summoned," Ayala said, her eyes dancing with pride and pleasure she gestured toward the dais.

Kiya followed the line of Ayala's hand and found herself locking eyes with the King himself before she could stop herself. The audacity of the eye contact didn't appear to bother the man upon the throne, however, as he beckoned to her with a faint smile.

Dropping her eyes demurely, as a proper woman should, Kiya rose and walked to the base of the three steps. There, she sank to her knees and bowed her head. "You wished to speak to me, Pharaoh?" she asked, aware that the eyes of every noble and courtier in the room were upon her again, though they felt far less forgiving and admiring this time.

"Come," the King said. "Sit beside me."

Kiya looked up again in surprise and saw him indicated a thick cushion on the stone beside the throne that Kiya was quite certain had not been there before. After a second's hesitation, and not wanting to anger the King, Kiya got to her feet and ascended the steps. A flurry of whispers started up as a counterpoint to the renewal of the music as she reached the top of the dais and stood before the King.

Careful to avoid looking the Son of Horus directly in the eye again, Kiya bowed and then moved to sit upon the cushion, folding her long, muscular legs up beneath her. She prayed that the pounding of her heart wasn't as loud as it seemed to her to be as she reached up to remove her mask, setting it carefully beside her.

"Here. You must be thirsty after your hunt," the King said, his smile audible as he held a cup of wine out for her.

Scandalized to be served thusly by the King himself, Kiya almost looked up at him, but held herself in check. She *was* thirsty, and, after all, she would now miss out on the meal that the other dancers would be partaking of off to the side of the hall where they would be out of the way of the nobles. Kiya reluctantly took the cup, a simple but elegant piece carved of ivory so delicate it was almost translucent. The wine it contained was fine and sweet and of a much better vintage than her fellow dancers would be drinking at this moment. The cool liquid was almost sensual as it slid down her throat and she began to feel the effects of the alcohol almost immediately.

"Thank you, Pharaoh," Kiya said softly after that first sip.

"You are welcome," came the reply and Kiya chanced another look up at him when she felt that he was no longer watching her.

He was younger than she'd expected, looking as though he was perhaps a few years older than Kiya, herself, was. When one ignored the crown, he was also rather… well, *ordinary looking*, she realized, shocked with herself for thinking such things about the son of a god.

That wasn't to say that he wasn't handsome, of course, she added silently, attempting to mitigate the disrespect of her thoughts. Her mother had always cautioned her to be more mindful of her opinions, even those she expressed only to herself. *Especially* those, for the gods, as her mother was fond of reminding her, were always listening.

His face was hard and angular, much the sort of face she would expect of a king or a general, his skin tanned from the sun and there were small lines around his dark eyes from squinting in the glare of the desert. He was on the tall side and slender, but wiry and lean rather than weak; Kiya had no doubt that his slight build was deceptive and that he was probably much stronger than he looked.

"Your eyes are lovely," the King said suddenly, turning to face her and catching her gaze again. "Very unusual."

Kiya flushed a bit and dropped her gaze once more. Her eyes, a rich, deep blue like the ocean, had long been a source of embarrassment. They marked her as different, and many considered them a source of shame for her family as it was visible proof that her great-great-grandfather had taken a barbarian from the green western lands as his bride. "Thank you," she managed, and then attempted to hide her discomfiture behind taking a sip from her cup of wine.

"You are embarrassed," he said and Kiya was appalled to feel the tips of his fingers press against the underside of her jaw, gently forcing her to look up. "Why?" She was surprised to see genuine curiosity in his expression, not judgment or animosity.

Kiya shrugged a little, the smallest lift of one shoulder. "They are an inconvenient reminder that I have barbarian blood," she admitted, her voice almost too quiet to be heard over the sound of the ongoing banquet.

"They mark you as different," the King observed and nodded a little, his expression thoughtful. "Tell me…" he paused. "What is your name?"

"Kiya, Pharaoh," Kiya replied, wishing she could melt into the floor and escape the audience.

"Kiya, do you think it is bad to be different?" the King asked, studying her. "Do you think that you are less of a person, or even less of an Egyptian, because of your heritage?"

"Of course not," Kiya replied, rather more sharply than she'd intended at the implication, her gaze snapping upward again.

Rather than taking offense, the King surprised her by smiling. "Then why do you care what fools think?" he asked, his tone almost playful as he challenged her.

Taken aback, Kiya simply stared at him, having no immediate answer for that question. "I… suppose I should not," she said after a moment.

"That's right," the King said, looking out at the other nobles with an expression that lent the comments greater significance. "You *should not*."

"Pharaoh?" Kiya asked, her tone uncertain.

The King looked back at her and smiled gently. "Never mind," he said, his tone warm. "I simply fear I have been too long among my fellow nobles."

Kiya smiled a little at that before she could stop herself. "I see."

The King raised an eyebrow, his smile widening into a grin. "Do you? I suppose you must find all this very amusing in some ways," he said, indicating the mass of feasters and the trappings of the event. "Speak plainly now, Kiya. I wish an honest opinion."

Caught! Kiya heard her mother in her mind. *This is why you should have more care with your words,* the scolding voice continued. However, now he was looking at her expectantly. "I am sure that my opinion would mean little, Pharaoh. I have only attended such functions as an entertainer and, I believe, lack the proper perspective."

The King's smile faded quickly and Kiya felt her heart sink. "Well... now, that is a good and properly diplomatic answer, though I am quite certain I asked for honesty over diplomacy," he reminded her.

Kiya was dismayed to realize that she felt ashamed at the disappointment she saw in his eyes. "My apologies, Pharaoh," she said softly.

"Do you fear me, Kiya?" The King asked after a moment, his tone difficult for her to read.

Kiya frowned. *Did* she fear him? She considered for a moment, then decided the answer was "no." After a short time in his presence, she realized, she had started to see him as a man, rather than the son of a god. It was this more than the man himself who caused her to fear.

Finally, she answered "You are the Pharaoh, the son of Horus, brought forth into the world to lead our nation. It is only right that a commoner such as I should fear you."

"And yet, you do not," he replied, his smile returning to his tone. "Good. Fear has its place and its uses, but I would not have you fear me."

Kiya looked up at him with surprise. "Pharaoh?" she asked again, confused.

In response, the King reached out to stroke her hair gently, almost tenderly. "When we are speaking like this, I would like for you to call me Menat," he said, looking into her eyes. "That is the name my mother gave me."

Part of Kiya tried to recoil at the intimacy implied by such a request, but she could not. As much as Kiya felt she should find this wrong, she realized that she *liked* Menat, in spite of his being the Pharaoh. "As you wish... Menat," she said after a moment, earning another warm smile.

The smile warmed his dark eyes and softened the hard angles of his face. "Good. I would like to ask a favor of you," he said, watching her once more.

Kiya inclined her head. "I am at your disposal, Pha- - Menat," she said.

"I would like you to watch," Menat said, indicating the rest of the nobles with a small movement of his wrist, "and tell me what you see."

"I am not sure I understand what you mean," Kiya admitted after a moment.

Quests & Answers

"I would like your impressions, if you will, of the noblemen and women of my court. More than that, I will not say. I would prefer to avoid tainting your perceptions with my own," Menat told her, still watching her.

Kiya nodded slowly. "I will do my best," she said, looking out over the gathered nobles again.

"I know that you will," Menat assured her.

Kiya and Menat subsided into a surprisingly companionable silence as the banquet continued. Moments after the King was brought a plate of food, he heard Kiya's stomach rumble (much to her consternation) and quietly ordered a servant to make up a plate for her as well. Although she was galled by her stomach's betrayal, Menat's kindness was a pleasant surprise, indeed.

And so, Kiya watched, resolving to be particularly vigilant in her duties as observer. She was surprised to find that she wanted very much to please Menat and to impress him with her insights into the court. However, she was dismayed to find that much of what she saw disturbed her. Many of the men and women sworn to serve Menat seemed to be mocking him in their conversations, judging by how they would laugh softly among themselves, watching to make sure he wasn't looking in their direction.

The lasciviousness, she expected. As a commoner and a dancer for the higher ranks, she had been groped more than once. It was an expected, if unwelcome, side-effect of the combination of alcohol, power, and mostly-naked flesh. However, she did not expect to find the nobles so blatantly displaying such avarice toward one another, and toward the king. She watched as one mother coached a daughter of no more than thirteen years before sending her to pay respects to Menat, and adjusting the girl's fine gown so that it hung from her shoulders, nearly showing the child's entire budding bosom!

Kiya watched the girl with silent sympathy as the child was scolded for attempting to right the gown. The girl brought a gift of a *senet* set which was beautifully carved from turquoise and obsidian. The game board's thirty squares alternated between turquoise with obsidian glyphs and obsidian with turquoise inlaid. The two sets of tokens were also both made of the two stones and the counting sticks for determining the number of moves to be made were made of intricately carved teak wood. Kiya focused on her plate, trying to avoid adding to the girl's humiliation; her cheeks already burned scarlet as she stammered out her rehearsed greeting for Menat.

Kiya couldn't make out much of what the girl actually said, and she wasn't sure that Menat did either, but his voice when he responded was kind and warm. "Thank you for your generous gift, Sama," he said. Kiya was impressed with the fact that he would remember the girl's name when there were so many noble families who, no doubt, had young sons and daughters that were brought to court. "It will be well used, I assure you. My old senet set is all but falling apart," he added with a chuckle which seemed to put the girl at ease somewhat as she bowed and took her leave.

"Kiya, will you set this beside you?" he asked her as the girl withdrew.

Kiya looked up to take the senet set and nodded. It truly was a beautiful set with each square perfectly cut from the stone and the symbols of the game board inlaid in the opposite color so that the turquoise squares had obsidian glyphs and the obsidian squares had turquoise glyphs. "It is beautiful," she said softly as she set it on the stone beside her cushion.

"Yes," Menat replied, though Kiya thought he sounded troubled.

She ventured another look up at him and found subtle signs that her instinct was correct. "Is everything alright?" she asked softly.

Menat looked over at her and favored her with a small smile. "Yes, of course," he assured her, the warmth returning to his expression. "Now, tell me what you have observed."

The invitation, though warmly delivered, caused Kiya's stomach to sink to somewhere around the vicinity of her ankles. She chewed her lip lightly, considering her answer carefully before responding. Remembering the disappointment she saw in him when she attempted diplomacy, she braced herself and said "The nobles do not seem to respect you very much. They whisper behind their hands and laugh when you are not looking in their direction. That seems to be occurring more frequently the longer I remain here, so I can only assume that they're wondering about my presence as well, and what function I am to serve for you."

Menat nodded slowly. "I can only imagine what those ideas must be," he said, shaking his head a little. A sly smile appeared on his face again as he added

"Perhaps I should appoint you a royal adviser. Imagine the consternation that would provoke."

His laughter was so infectious that Kiya found herself joining in before she realized it. "That would be putting it mildly, I suspect," she replied, catching several unfriendly glances from various courtiers.

As the laughter trailed off, the sound of musical bells rang through the hall as the chamberlain stepped to the fore of the dais. "Lords and Ladies, the Pharaoh thanks you all for your presence and your kind gifts. May the gods protect you as you make your way home this night," he intoned, his voice ringing through the hall and drawing the occasion to a close.

Kiya watched as the courtiers finished their last cups of wine and beer and then rise from their cushions to begin leaving the palace. After a few moments, she looked at the Pharaoh without meeting his eyes. "Thank you for your kindness, Pharaoh," she said politely, keeping her eyes focused on the pectoral resting on his chest and shoulders to prevent the temptation of looking into his eyes.

It rose and fell as he sighed. "Thank you for keeping me company, Kiya. I enjoyed our talk very much."

Kiya's smile was shy as she nodded, her bold streak coming to the fore again as she said "If ever I can be of service to the Pharaoh again, I am at your disposal."

Another warm chuckle came from the man in response to that. "I may take you up on that," he said as he rose from his seat.

Kiya watched him go, and then turned to hurry down the steps of the dais toward the antechamber where her fellow dancers would be waiting for her. She had no doubt that she would be the subject of as much, if not more, curiosity from them as she received from the courtiers.

Kiya.

Her hand was actually on the door, preparing to push it aside when she stopped dead in her tracks. Turning her head slightly, she saw men and women moving around the hall, cleaning up the mess left behind by the banquet, but no one seemed to be looking at her and she saw no indication that any of them had called to her. Shaking her head a little, she started to push on the door when she heard it again.

Kiya. It was a woman's voice, but it was deep and resonant rather than strident and scolding as her mother's voice usually sounded in her mind. *I have need of you.*

"Where are you?" Kiya asked, looking around again. A young man with skin so dark it was almost the color of ebony wood gave her a disapproving frown, but said nothing.

Come. This way, quickly, the voice said and she was finally able to locate it near the entrance to the corridor that the Pharaoh had left down. She saw the shape of a tall woman beckoning to her, though she couldn't quite make out the details of the woman's appearance.

Turning from the door and walking cautiously toward the woman. Once the figure saw Kiya approaching her, she turned to precede her down the corridor. Treading lightly and looking around, worried that someone was going to stop her and demand to know what she was doing here.

Following the mysterious woman, Kiya gradually realized that she was deep into the area of the palace where Menat and his family resided. The thought made her steps falter as outright terror at being caught and punished kicked in. However, she saw another figure quickly cross the crossing corridor ahead, moving in a hunched, hurried way that triggered her suspicion and got her moving again.

She reached the corner and peered around the corner to see the middle aged man, a servant she remembered seeing at the banquet, working with the chamberlain. As she peeked, she saw him turn into a room on the right side of the corridor.

Hurry, Kiya, the mysterious voice said, the urgency of it quickening her steps and she realized she was almost running by the time she reached the doorway.

Inside, the room she saw Menat standing near the windows, reading a scroll. The chamberlain's man approached, his presence noted with a bare glance in his direction from the Pharaoh. "Place it on the table there," he said, his tone distracted as the man approached.

Kiya had no idea what the man was supposed to be delivering, but what she saw was a wickedly sharp blade sliding from its sheath as the man approached Menat's unguarded back. Her eyes widened and she didn't need the unknown voice urging her (*Stop him!*) to put her into motion. Crossing from the door to the servant in a few long strides, she cried out "Menat, look out!" as she grabbed for the wrist of the hand holding the knife.

The look of shock on Menat's face as he turned to see not only the chamberlain's man holding a blade, but

Quests & Answers

also struggling with Kiya evaporated quickly as he crossed over to assist her. Unarmed as he was, he was undaunted as he drew back his fist and slammed it into the older man's cheek.

The effect was instantaneous and dramatic. The blade fell from the servant's hand and he went limp, crumpling to the floor, taking Kiya with him as she failed to release him. She heard Menat shout for the guards, then felt strong hands grip her upper arms to pull her to her feet.

"Kiya, are you alright?"

The figure she saw beyond Menat's shoulder held Kiya's rapt attention. The goddess Sekhmet, wrapped in her crimson and gold gown watched them from near the window, the firelight dancing in her gold eyes. As she saw Kiya watching her, the feline lips pulled up and back into a smile and she inclined her head, her hand over her heart. *Come to my temple at midday, Kiya. I have need of a strong, brave woman such as you,* the mysterious voice said in her mind. With a jolt, she recognized that it was, in fact, Sekhmet, the mighty goddess of warfare and vengeance, speaking to her.

She managed to nod before the goddess faded from sight and found herself looking into the worried eyes of the king. "Are you hurt?" he asked again, clearly concerned by her lack of response to his inquiries.

"I am fine," Kiya assured him as the guards and the royal physician came hurrying into the chambers.

Menat's shoulders visibly relaxed as she finally replied and he turned to look toward the fallen man, allowing her to see the guards haul him to his feet to take him away. She also saw the blade which was black and pitted, the hilt carved into a horrific serpent motif.

"Don't touch that," Kiya surprised herself by commanding, as one of the guards reached for it.

All the men looked toward her, aghast at being ordered by a girl, and a commoner at that, but their consternation turned to horror as the snake that formed the dagger's hilt came alive and tried to bite the guard's outstretched hand. With a cry of revulsion, the guard staggered back, while one of his fellows drew his blade and brought the edge down hard on the evil thing, snapping it in two and sending a wash of black ichor across the sandstone floor.

The looks of anger and confusion then turned to fear and suspicion as the guardsmen looked at Kiya.

"How did you know that would happen, Kiya?" Menat asked, his tone gentle and curious more than anything else.

Realizing how mad the truth would sound, Kiya shook her head and broke away from Menat, pelting out of the room and back the way she came. She found her way back to the others of the troop in moments. Ignoring the jibes and teasing for her meal with the Pharaoh, she subsided into silence as they loaded into the two carts to ride back to the Hathor temple to wash up before returning to their homes.

Ayala reached over to take her hand, concern in her dark eyes once she got Kiya to look up to meet her gaze. "What is wrong? Surely their taunts have not stung you that deeply...?"

Kiya chewed her lip lightly and shook her head. "Ayala, I need to go to the temple of Sekhmet tomorrow. Will you come with me?"

Quests & Answers

Ayala blinked in surprise. "I thought you said the priestesses had visited your home already."

"They did," Kiya confirmed, remembering the sting of the casual dismissal once they'd seen her blue eyes. "Sekhmet spoke to me this evening, though. She has commanded that I go."

Ayala looked shocked, as one would expect, and watched Kiya for a long moment as though trying to determine if it was now her turn to be made fun of. Ultimately, however, she saw no mockery and slowly nodded. "Yes, I will go with you," she assured Kiya, giving her friend's hand a gentle squeeze. "You truly believe that you have been called to be Sekhmet's Light?" she asked in a soft, awed tone.

"I know that I have been called to try," Kiya replied quietly, returning the squeeze. In truth, she had no idea what the next day would bring, but she knew that as long as Ayala believed in her, she could do anything.

The next day just before midday, the two young women met and hurried to the temple district of the city. As they neared the complex containing the temples dedicated to Sekhmet, Ptah and their son, Nefertem, Kiya's sense that this was the right course of action intensified. As the patron gods of the city, these were the largest and most elaborate of the temples constructed in the city and the area around them was very busy with worshipers and priests and priestesses coming and going.

The girls' pace slowed as they neared the path to Sekhmet's temple, its length lined with statuary of her sacred lionesses, and Kiya took Ayala's hand. Ayala smiled reassuringly at her friend, but continued to hold Kiya's hand as they walked. After ascending the steps to the front doors, Kiya spotted a group of priestesses nearby, talking in the shade of an awning.

Looking over at Ayala, Kiya gave her a slight smile. "Wish me luck," she said softly, leaning in to kiss her friend's cheek.

Ayala kissed Kiya in return and smiled. "You do not need luck," she replied firmly, finally withdrawing her hand. "I will stay here until you are inside."

Kiya nodded, remaining beside her for a moment, and then turning to walk toward the women. She was only a few feet away when her approach was finally noticed and the priestesses turned toward her.

"Yes, child," the youngest of them asked though she was likely no more than five years older than Kiya, herself.

Looking at the calm expressions of mild curiosity, Kiya swallowed, then said "Sekhmet spoke to met last night and told me I should come here."

The expressions on the women's faces went from mild curiosity to incredulity. The priestess who'd spoken narrowed her eyes slightly and moved a bit closer to Kiya. "What is your name, child? Do you live nearby?"

Kiya rankled at the condescending tone, but bit her temper back as she answered the woman. "My name is Kiya, and I live a few miles south of here."

"Oh, yes... I remember you, now," the youngest priestess said, eyeing Kiya critically. "I spoke to your mother during our search for Sekhmet's champion. I determined that you were unsuitable."

"You determined?" Kiya asked, her tone becoming incredulous. "How did you determine that when you never even *spoke* to me?"

"Sacmis, what is the problem?" one of the older priestesses asked.

The young woman, Sacmis, looked back at the older priestess. "A candidate appears to believe she is above my judgment of her worthiness."

"When you presume to know me and my capabilities without ever meeting me, yes, I suppose I do," Kiya retorted, her tone sharper than she'd intended it to be.

"Perhaps she has a point, Sacmis," the eldest of the priestesses said in a reasonable tone. "Although much can be learned of a candidate by speaking to the family, it is always best to speak to the young woman directly."

Sacmis made a dismissive sound. "I did not *need* to speak to her. One look told me all I needed to know. She is unworthy of Sekhmet's regard," she snapped, gesturing toward Kiya's face.

"Barbarian blood," one of the others added in a tone that said she agreed.

"Even so, we have been searching for three years and found no one the goddess deems suitable. Should we discount a possibility so blithely?" another asked.

Sacmis rounded on the dissenter. "How *dare* you accuse me of shirking my duties," she snapped.

Kiya watched in dismay as the priestesses descended into bickering, her own presence apparently forgotten. A hand on her arm startled her, pulling her attention away from the argument to see the eldest priestess, the one who had first questioned Sacmis' dismissal of Kiya, standing beside her.

"I am Asenet," the priestess said, her tone kind and reassuring. "Come with me and I will see to your preparation to go before the goddess."

Kiya ventured a small smile. "You believe me?"

Asenet smiled in return, placing a hand on Kiya's back to guide her along. "I believe that you should have been tested to begin with, so perhaps the goddess did come to you. She may have become impatient with our mortal efforts and taken matters into her own hands."

Kiya nodded and looked back toward the other priestesses who were still arguing among themselves. "What about them?"

Asenet chuckled softly. "They will figure it out eventually," she said as she pushed the door to the temple open to bring Kiya inside. "Come, let us prepare you. I believe that you're in for a grand adventure."

Ayala watched from her place at the top of the steps as the door closed behind Kiya, a small, sad smile on her lips. "Goodbye, my friend...." she whispered, and then turned to go.

Jill's Run
By Garth Reasby

Author's Note: *Although she's a minor player in the first novel of the Children of Divinity series, Jill's personality is far larger than one small role could ever contain. This story takes place during the events of Awaken, and tells how she went from being in protective custody to showing up in London for the climax of the novel.*

* * * * *

I'm done. Don't call me.

The words struck Jill like a punch to the stomach. Nausea made her stomach flip flop and breathing felt uncomfortably difficult. Her lower lip started quivering, so Jill bit it lightly in a futile attempt to make it stop. The young woman's knuckles turned white as she clutched her cell phone and reread the message. Before she could set the device aside Jill's Facebook application let her know that she had been unfriended by Marty Dean. The happy little beep that accompanied the message made her feel like she was being mocked. For a second she considered heaving the phone into the wall but refrained and just dropped it on the bed next to her while sighing heavily. It didn't help. None of it did. Her life was over.

Jill brushed her fingers near the corners of her eyes and felt them come away wet. She hadn't been seeing Marty very long but he was funny and sensitive and an incredible artist. In her seventeen year old world the month and a half long relationship was a lifetime. Jill sighed loudly. Then she growled.

"God damn it, Jordan. Damn you and your fucking men in black."

The trick to turning grief into anger, as Jill had found, was finding a focus. She hated being angry but it seemed like it hurt less than feeling the heart rending pain of a breakup. For the moment she directed that anger at her older sister Jordan. Her sister the spy. Jill never believed Jordan's stories of being just a security analyst. She always imagined her eldest sibling leaping from crashing planes or out running bad guys in her sleek Mercedes SLR sports car. Jordan was too aggressive and too action oriented to just travel around and conduct security inspections. No, the eldest sister of the Law clan was neck deep in espionage and Jill wouldn't accept any other truth.

With a dramatic flail of her arms Jill flopped onto her back and stared at the spinning ceiling fan above her. The adrenaline that accompanied her anger vanquished the nausea and made Jill feel supercharged. It wouldn't last and Jill knew it. Eventually she would have to just deal with the loss but that time wasn't now. Now she was furious and all Jill could think about was being pulled from the rave less than twenty four hours ago.

Quests & Answers

******

The music beats hit hard and fast in a rhythm that was hypnotic. The thudding base was a heartbeat for the organism comprised of nearly two hundred of Britain's young adults. Tonight it was in an old shipping warehouse at the docks. Nobody came down to the old place so it was perfect for what was essentially an illegal party.

In the span of a few short hours the rave's organizers had installed a variety of strobe and colored lights and rolled in a powerful sound system to churn out music. Flyers notifying the ravers had gone out a few days ago but the secret location had been kept until only two hours before the start. At a specified time the website run by the organizers was updated to provide the location. It took less than fifteen minutes for the crowd to start building.

Jill was dressed in a too-short black skirt and a too-small pink Hello Kitty half top that she knew her parents wouldn't approve of. She had meticulously put glittering scales along her legs, sides, neck and arms and then donned a variety of neon colored light bracelets. After a trip to the salon to get a pixie cut Jill added vibrant pink streaks through her normally blonde locks and a dash of sparkles. The look was typical for a rave but not the daughter of a well-bred family.

Unlike many of the other ravers Jill wasn't under the influence of any drug or alcohol. This isn't to say she hadn't had alcohol, but her body's ability to rapidly heal purged it as fast as it would any other poison. Jill wasn't sure how her body healed so quickly or seemed to be immune to the effects of alcohol. In movies people like her were locked up. They were experimented on, and hidden away in secret labs by mad scientists. Jill had given up on learning how her gifts worked long ago. She was just out to enjoy them now.

Any further thoughts were driven away by the cool touch of a freshly filled plastic cup being pressed into her hand. Jill smiled brightly at the young man who had brought it, Marty Dean.

Marty was tall and a bit on the thin side, but he was attractive in a gothy sort of way. Jill thought that he had the most amazing smile- even if it was rare to see. Marty's tousled black hair, cut to make him look edgy and dangerous, only made her appreciate his looks more. He was dressed in typical goth fashion with leather pants and a black t-shirt and heavy biker boots on his feet.

"I thought you could use another." Marty said. Despite how loudly he spoke, Jill still had to lean close to hear it over the music.

"Oh, I can." Jill replied. She nearly had to shout her reply though the way Marty craned his neck Jill assumed he hadn't heard her. Instead of shouting again she winked and leaned up to kiss his cheek. He smelled as if he had quite a few drinks already, though Jill didn't mind. The more he drank the more outgoing Marty became and the more amorous, so in Jill's opinion it was a win-win scenario.

Marty favored Jill with another smile and started leading her towards the packed dance floor. Jill hurriedly downed her drink and allowed herself to be led into the mash of sweaty, undulating bodies. She

32   *Quests & Answers*

wasted no time in joining them and allowed herself to be drawn into the hypnotic embrace of the music.

The couple remained on the dance floor for a good hour before they stepped outside to get some air. This time Jill led Marty, the gravity of Jill's excitement pulling Marty with it. An exuberant smile dominated Jill's face. The frenetic energy that fed her expression invigorated every step to a point that it was a near bounce. Almost as soon as they pass through the door Jill turned and kissed Marty utilizing that same energy in a more passionate endeavor. Before Jill could truly begin to enjoy the moment someone cleared their throat from behind her.

Without removing her arms from around Marty Jill looked in direction of the sound. Three men wearing black suits looked very out of place amongst the parking area full of rave kids. The tallest of the men, a handsome Caucasian man with impeccably arrayed black hair, stepped forward and produced a black leather wallet from his inside pocket. He flipped it open to reveal a government ID, "Ms. Law. I'm Agent Shaw of MI6. I need you to come with me." The man's business like tone was polite and he gestured for Jill to head towards the parking area with one hand.

For a moment Jill wondered if this were some joke but then she beckoned towards the hand holding the ID wallet, "Let me see that."

Patiently the man held the wallet closer so Jill could see the ID better. Jill took her time reading the details to ensure that the ID was like Jordan's. In the meantime Marty had moved to stand next to Jill so he could glower at the men properly.

Marty's words were slightly slurred, though an unmistakable bluster colored his tone, "What's this about then?"

Agent Shaw met Marty's eyes, "I can't discuss it with you, Mr. Dean. Ms. Law, we need to go," If the young man's tone or state of inebriation had any impact on Shaw he didn't show it.

Jill frowned and stepped back, her hands closing around Marty's bicep, "Is my sister alright?"

Shaw nodded briefly and tucked his ID back into his suit pocket, "She's perfectly fine, Ms. Law. However, we need to put you into protective custody. There's a situation that we're taking care of…"

Empowered by the confidence of a few to many drinks Marty cut agent Shaw off, "Then take care of it mate. We're alright here. "

The tall agent quirked an eyebrow but kept his tone polite and even, "Mr. Dean. This matter doesn't concern you. I suggest you go back inside and enjoy the party."

"I said shove off," Marty retorted rudely. "You wankers aren't wanted round here. Take your jackboots and go bother some terrorist or something."

Half way to titillation Jill struggled to keep a smile off of her face. She enjoyed Marty's protectiveness and for better or worse let him continue.

"Mr. Dean, you've clearly had too much to drink, but this is the last polite response you're going to get. Move along *please*," Shaw said in a firmer tone of voice. His eyes remained focused on Marty's as redirected his verbal attention, "Ms. Law, I'm sorry that we have to cut your night short but we need to go."

34   *Quests & Answers*

"Look," Marty put his hand against Shaw's chest and pushed hard, "I said shove off."

Shaw wore a perturbed expression as he was pushed backwards. The agents to his left and right started to move in but Shaw shook his head, "I'm not in the habit of beating up children, Mr. Dean, but I *will* put you in jail for a few days."

Jill blinked as things suddenly turned physical between her boyfriend and the agent. The fact that Marty was ready to take on a guy who was much larger than he was excited Jill, but she realized what her boyfriend was up against. She had seen Jordan put three guys on their asses in the span of a second, and this guy was a lot bigger than she was. Jill put her hand on Marty's shoulder, "Wait a second."

Full of ire and booze Marty ignored Jill and lunged towards Shaw with his hand outstretched, "Fuck you. You don't know who my dad is, do you?"

The young man reached forward to curl his fingers into Shaw's pristine white shirt, a look of outrage on his young face. Only Marty knew what his intent had been in the action and that's how it would remain. Shaw exploded into action and grabbed Marty's fingers with one hand. Practiced and fluid, Agent Shaw peeled the offending digits back from his chest and twisted hard. He followed the motion through by rotating the young man's arm at the shoulder and extending it, bending his hand back towards his shoulder.

The unexpected response forced Marty to either go to one knee or have his shoulder dislocated and like most people with an aversion to pain he complied. His capitulation was accompanied by a yelp of pain and the instinctual response of trying to pull his arm free, "That hurts!"

Shaw tightened the hold and made Marty cry out again, "I understand you want to look good for your girlfriend; this isn't the way to do it."

Marty made an attempt to pull away from Shaw, but the effort made his shoulder wrench again, "Let go of me!"

"We're past that point, "Shaw said and hauled Marty to his feet. Using the momentum he maneuvered the young man's arm behind him and handed him off to the agent to his right, "Send him to the Met and tell them to cool him overnight."

"Do you have to?" Jill asked, her tone flirting with anger, "He's drunk."

"He is. He's also stupid but I doubt a night enjoying the hospitality of the Metropolitan Police is going to fix that," Shaw answered and motioned for Jill to follow him. This time the agent turned for the parking lot and didn't wait for Jill to agree with him.

"Fuck you, cunts!" Marty growled as the two agents cuffed him up.

After glancing at Marty, Jill hurried up next to Shaw and started to put a hand on his arm, "I'll go with you just don't put him in jail. His dad thinks we're studying."

Shaw didn't pause and headed straight towards a black Range Rover that idled nearby. He nodded to the amused looking agent behind the wheel and pulled the rear passenger side door open, "Ms. Law, we aren't negotiating. Get in."

Quests & Answers

Jill sighed loudly and folded her arms, "Not until you let Marty go."

Shaw and the dark skinned agent that sat behind the wheel of the rover exchanged looks. The latter smiled and shrugged his shoulders, "She did warn you."

"That she did," Shaw replied dryly.

"Who did?" Jill asked incredulously, "Jordan?"

Shaw pointed to the inside of the vehicle, "Get in, Ms. Law"

Jill frowned, "Will you stop calling me that, it makes me sound old. What did Jordan say about me?"

"That you were stubborn," Shaw replied and gently placed a hand on Jill's back to prompt her to get in the waiting SUV, "Now if you don't mind."

"I'm not stubborn," Jill protested but did as she was told. She looked to see where Marty was and frowned angrily when she saw him cuffed up.

The young man was being escorted to a second SUV by the other two agents, cursing all the way. He tried to break free again and then spit in one man's face. That seemed to be the limit of the man's patience and he punched Marty in the side so hard that the boy doubled over in pain. Marty's mouth gasped like a fish as he tried to suck in air. His legs gave out entirely and the agents let him fall onto the dusty gravel parking lot. The formerly argumentative man was clearly in a lot of pain as he rolled from side to side moaning. The man that had punched Marty hauled back his fist to strike him again, fully intent on making sure the lesson was learned.

Jill gasped and bolted towards Marty but Shaw caught her arm before she had taken more than two steps, "Let go of me, God damn it!"

"Robison!" Shaw barked, "Back off." The commanding tone in his voice gave the other agent pause and he lowered his hand.

"I said let go!" Jill growled and jerked her arm in a vain attempt to free it.

Shaw met Jill's eyes which caused her to stop struggling, "Go ahead," he said and released her.

There was no hesitation as Jill hurried to Marty and knelt down next to him. She didn't care if she got dirty and reached out to touch Marty's side. Jill looked at where the man had punched Marty and focused on it. The world immediately came alive with an array of colors. Most of Marty's body was covered in an aura of blue the color of the sky. The area that the agent had punched was dark orange bordering on red, and Jill could see the orange spreading outwards from the point of impact. It was a turning into a bruise but nothing that was life threatening. Jill caught the faint scent of urine and realized that the man had hit Marty so hard that he lost control of his bladder.

Jill looked at Shaw accusingly, "What the fuck was that?"

"It'll be handled," Shaw promised and walked over to where Marty lay on the ground. He looked Robison in the eyes and nodded towards the first SUV, "You're driving."

The driver of the first SUV slid out from behind the wheel and walked towards where Marty lay. He and Robison exchanged looks as they passed but said nothing. The dark skinned agent nodded to Jill and carefully lifted Marty to his feet, "I'm agent Laird. I'll make sure he gets looked at."

"You expect me to trust any of you after that? All you did was prove Marty was right," Jill snarled and speared Shaw with a nasty glare, "I'm going to the hospital with him."

"No you're not," Shaw said and watched Laird put Marty in the back of the second SUV, "I'm sorry for what my man did but it doesn't change anything. We have to get you to a safe location. Once we're there I'll be able to explain what's going on."

"And if I refuse are you going to let that asshole hit me too?" Jill said and squared off with Shaw.

"Of course not Ms. Law but I will put you over my shoulder if that's what it takes."

Jill growled and turned towards the SUV where Marty was being secured but Shaw grabbed her bicep. She whirled on the agent ready to punch him but the patient look in his eyes stopped her. After a moment she lowered her fist and sighed, "Fine."

"Thank you, Ms. Law," Agent Shaw replied quietly and gestured towards the SUV.

"Jill," She replied and stalked towards the Range Rover's open door, "Not Jillian, or Ms. Law, just Jill."

"Jill," Shaw confirmed.

Reluctantly Jill pulled herself into the SUV's back seat, immediately folding her arms. When the driver looked at her through the rear view mirror Jill glared at him icily. She was about to chastise the agents again when she caught Shaw's thoughtful expression in profile. The man was trying to hide it but the tightness around his eyes and the set of his jaw spoke volumes to her. He was angry. Jill concentrated and let her perceptions shift so that she could see the flow of his energy. Skin gave way to bone and muscle, robust organs, and a vast network of blood vessels and capillaries. Adrenaline was saturating his body, but so were a variety of other hormones and chemicals. With his body mostly obscured by the seat Jill couldn't see everything going on in Agent Shaw. What drew her attention was the series of angry orange and red flares haloing the man's Amygdala. The almond shaped portion of Shaw's brain was full of emotion, mostly anger. Those energy arcs flared brightly as Shaw turned his gaze on the man he had called Robison and Jill immediately recognized the association.

At least you're not a total bastard.

The fact that Shaw's reaction had redeemed him somewhat didn't stop Jill from voicing her mind. Little usually did, "You know this is bullshit, right?"

Shaw looked over his shoulder at Jordan's youngest sister, his expression neutral, "Lots in things in life are. You'll get used to it."

******

A sharp knock on the door abruptly pulled Jill out of the past. She wiped at the corner of her eyes and cheeks where tears were winding their way along her skin before glancing at the door. A second knock hurried Jill's response, "What!?"

Quests & Answers

The door opened slowly and Jill's sister Marisa peered in. The inquisitive look in her blue eyes wasn't what Jill was expecting, "Hey."

Jill's tone softened, "Hey."

Marisa pushed her fingers through her blonde hair and tucked it behind her right ear. It was an attempt to soften her look some. Jill had seen it before, but it wasn't common. Marisa seldom felt the need to do it for Jill's benefit. The two were only four years apart in age and it always seemed that they fought more often than not. It had been that way for as long as Jill could remember and had only gotten worse once Marisa had become a police officer.

The two sisters watched one another in silence. "I wanted to see how you were doing. I heard you were set off when you came up here." Marisa finally said. Without invitation, Marisa stepped into the room shutting the door behind her.

A shrug was Jill's response and she pushed into a sitting position on her bed. Out of habit she drew her knees up and wrapped her arms around them. Marisa's expression became more sympathetic in response. *God damn it.* Jill swung her legs off of the bed abruptly and gave Marisa a hard look, "Stop reading me. Stop using your cop mojo on me."

Marisa's hands came up defensively, "It's habit. Besides, if your lower lip was jutted out any further you'd be poking me in the eye with it." She pulled her black leather jacket off and draped it over the back of Jill's desk chair before she sat on corner of the desk. Even in a pair of black slacks and a grey turtleneck Marisa radiated authority. "What happened?"

"He dumped me."

"Shit." Marisa's shoulders lost most of their tension. "I'm sorry, Jill." Marisa answered in a quiet voice.

Jill paced over to her window and looked out. Her tone was sharp, accusatory, "It's not *your* fault, Mari. It's *Jordan's*. "

Marisa watched Jill calmly, her hands settling on her slender hips, "Jill, you know she wouldn't intentionally hurt you."

A hiss of dismissal pushed between Jill's clenched teeth. Marisa was right but that rational part of Jill was submerged by teenaged hormones and heartache, "Fuck her."

Quietly, Marisa approached Jill and pulled her into a one armed hug, "Ease up now. I doubt Jordan even knows what happened."

Jill shrugged off Marisa's arm and turned to look up at her sister. Marisa was almost as tall as their older sisters and her sharp features tended to make her look stern. Jill stepped back a pace and frowned, "Yeah? So she doesn't even care enough to make sure we're all ok?"

"If she didn't' care we wouldn't all be locked up in protective custody."

Another hiss, though one of anger, came from Jill and she turned back to look out the window, "She just fucked up my entire life. I love Marty and now he hates me!"

Marisa's look was skeptical, "Really? You've been seeing him for what? A month? A month and a half?"

Here we go. Jill avoided Marisa's eyes, "It doesn't matter. You just know it when it happens. You may be content with a battery operated boyfriend but I'm not."

The bait wasn't taken and Marisa stayed on topic, "Jill, relax. I didn't come up here to argue with you. I heard you were really upset and I wanted to see if I could help." When Jill didn't respond Marisa sighed and walked over to collect her coat, "If you need anything I'll be in my room."

The sound of the door thumping shut in Marisa's wake made Jill's shoulders slump. Guilt added itself to Jill's emotional tapestry. For once Marisa was trying to be there for her and she had failed to take the offered hand. Sighing long and slow Jill rested her forehead against the window. She focused on the chill of the glass as it spread across her skin and used the sensation to dispel some of her stress.

A bright beam of light cutting across the yard intruded on Jill's attempt to repair her calm. Out in the garden behind the house Jill could see two of the security detail. One man was carrying a powerful flashlight in one hand while the other rested on his weapon. He swept the light around the large planters to dispel the shadows while his partner kept his attention focused on the larger area around them.

"HK G36K," Jill mused. Thanks to its use in several video games she enjoyed, she knew its' specs by heart. 5.56MM select fire, compact with a folding stock. This one had a 40mm grenade launcher on it as well. She noted that the other man was carrying a different sort of rifle, though this one she didn't recognize. It was black like the first, but sleek and the magazine was twice as thick.

Soon only the beam from the flashlight was visible as the men continued on, their black BDUs and matching combat gear rendering them ghostly silhouettes in the flashlight's beam.

Jill stood watching out the window for a while and saw another pair of figures come around. They were barely distinguishable from the darkness, little more than shadows stalking along the garden's stone paths. A smile formed on Jill's face and she grabbed a flashlight from her desk drawer. She depressed the button with her thumb which made the three rings of super bright light emitting diodes flare to life. Even through the glass window the beam illuminated the two figures making both of them flinch.

The unmistakable shape of night vision goggles over the two operator's faces caught Jill's eye. One made a short chopping motion with his hand, an effort to get her to shut off the light, and pushed up his goggles. She let the light remain on them for a few moments more so that she could see what else they were carrying. Each had a combat vest on and both were carrying those unfamiliar rifles in addition to a pistol in a tactical thigh holster. Jill saw they each had some sort of hand held optical sensors slung across their body armor. Though she didn't know for certain Jill guessed that they must be some sort of thermal sensor or motion detector.

Jill waved at the two and then shut off her flashlight. Smiling she sat at her laptop and brought up a web browser. "Let's start with hand held thermal scopes."

*****

A dark shadow crept quietly down the darkened hall. On tiptoe it crept past several closed doors, careful to not let the package it carried brush against their lacquered wooden surfaces. When the sound of male voices floated up the stairs from below the shadow froze. The volume grew as they closed in on where the shadow crouched next to the hall corner.

It waited, almost too afraid to breathe, blood rushing through its veins in hard, steady pulses. The volume of the voices rose so the shadow forced its breath to halt. Adrenaline fueled exhilaration laced the shadow's blood with energy which made its hands begin to shake. To make them stop the shade tucked its hands beneath the bent joints of its knees and waited.

Just as its lungs started to burn, the shade let its breath drift out in a slow barely audible exhalation. The voices continued in quiet unintelligible tones, apparently oblivious to the dark form that waited near the top landing of the stairs. After a few minutes the volume of their voices weakened as they drifted away from the base of the stairs.

The shadow surged up from its crouch and nimbly traversed the large staircase. It stuck to the side of the stair where it met the wall, avoiding the left that had numerous braces. Each brace was carved from the same oak that the doors and floor had been and were also lacquered to be slick and shiny. A space large enough for a house cat to sit was between each of wooden supports which allowed the lights of the living area below to shine into the stairs themselves, casting them in warm yellow glow.

As the shade reached the base of the stair it crouched again and listened, then pulled a cell phone from its pocket. Using its thumbs the shade pushed up the display and quickly hid it with a black gloved hand. Carefully the shade slid the phone around the corner and depressed a button on the side of the device. An artificial click whir played as the small device's built in camera triggered.

God damn it!

Jill cursed mentally and pulled the phone back, holding the screen against her chest. She used the black jacket to hide the glow from the display while her eyes darted back towards the living area. The sound of Jill's rapidly beating heart made her ear drums pulse and she wrinkled her nose at the unusual sensation. It wasn't as if she had never felt it before but it was different this time. She was so focused on being quiet that every sound her body made seemed to be so loud. In fact Jill wasn't sure how nobody had heard her yet. Jill tensed and took a slow, deep breath, trying to steady her hands in the process.

Hesitantly, Jill peered at the display, cupping one hand over the top to shield it. The image that camera had taken was blurry but clear enough for her to tell that the hall didn't have any guards in it. Just as she thought, they were focused on keeping people out of the house more than in. A fierce grin spread across Jill's face as the thrill of victory added to the adrenaline.

Isn't that premature?

The voice was Jordan's. It was as calm and proper as could be, giving no emotional cues as to the motive behind the question. Jill began to second guess all of her steps so far. The voice hadn't been real, just a memory of when Jordan had outsmarted her during a game of chess. At the time there was no doubt in Jill's mind that she had finally beaten her eldest sister but she had made one error, one flaw in her plan and Jordan destroyed her with it.

It was just a memory though. Wherever Jordan was, it wasn't here, in the family home. Jill's eyes narrowed as the emotions of losing Marty thanks to Jordan surfaced. Then Jill swatted it aside with a silent curse. She loved her sister, but Jill would be damned if she was going to let her life be run by others. The sound of boots on wood snapped Jill out of her reflection and sent her heart racing even faster.

The noise was coming from the living room where the security detail had set up their command center. There was no urgency to the pace of the footsteps but it wasn't a far walk to where Jill had concealed herself at the intersection of the two halls and the main foyer. Then she heard something else. A voice, warm and dulcet with a hint of playfulness. Marisa's voice. Temptation and Jill were well acquainted, not quite lovers but definitely more than friends. Like chocolate, Temptation easily bested Jill's will and she peered out from her hiding spot.

Marisa was sauntering along the hall with agent Shaw. Their pace was casual, and they were a bit closer together than two people who weren't well acquainted would stand. Marisa was dressed differently than before. A pair of tight black jeans hugged Marisa's hips and she had donned an all too familiar Hello Kitty shirt that was too small. The black material of shirt didn't quite reach Marisa's waist so it left a tantalizing amount of her toned midriff bare.

My shirt! She's using my shirt to land some guy and stretching the crap out of it!

Before Jill knew it she rose and started around the corner with her fists balled. After what Jordan had done there was no way Jill was going to allow Marisa to profit off of the presence of agent Shaw and his men, especially not in her favorite shirt.

Marisa saw Jill first and made eye contact with her. To Marisa's credit she kept her expression schooled and didn't alert agent Shaw to the fact that she had noticed her black clad sister storming around the corner.

You let your emotions get the better of you too often, Jill.

The youngest Law blinked as Jordan's voice admonished her again. Another memory, Jill observed. The context wasn't immediately clear but Jill quickly realized she had her fists balled so tightly that the joints of her fingers hurt. All the anger contained within Jill was about ready to burst out of her at the perceived transgression, and part of her anticipated the coming apocalypse she would create.

Great, my bloody inner monologue is Jordan.

"You know what? I think I left my mobile in the living room," Marisa said and started to turn around.

Shaw took his gaze from Marisa's face and glanced back the way they had come, "I'll go grab it for you." He smiled warmly and walked down the hall not noticing that Marisa's eyes had dropped lower to survey his rear.

"Thanks," Marisa replied, a pretty smile on her face. As soon as Shaw was off down the hall she looked back at Jill, her expression transforming into a stern mask. There was no sign of Jill. Without looking behind her, Jill darted around the opposite corner quickly, doing her best to keep her booted feet from making too much noise. She sped past the first two doors in the hall and ducked into the third on the right. As quietly as she could, Jill shut the door and turned her back to it. Before she could do anything else a massive dark form raised above her with its limbs extended. The weight of it held her fast and pressed Jill back into the door.

"No no no, no jumping." Jill hissed and failed to stop a smile from blossoming on her face.

The large Irish Wolfhound wasn't deterred and started to lick Jill's face, drawing its warm wet tongue from the underside of her jaw to her forehead. Its club like tail wagged enthusiastically and it moved in for a second lick.

Jill threw her hands in front of her face and wrinkled her nose, "Herne, no. Get off of me." Her voice was barely above a whisper, but the dog understood the tone and intent so it dropped down and looked up at her expectantly.

Soon Jill was surrounded by three other Wolfhounds as Herne's brother Camulus and their sisters Macha and Morrigan joined her by the door. In the dim light of what the family called 'The Dog Room' she could still make out their large shapes. The four large dogs were as big as Jill was and heavier. They could easily overpower her and Herne had knocked Jill to the floor more than once. Fortunately they were well-trained, even if Herne was a bit rebellious. With tails wagging the four all looked at Jill and waited.

"Ok, Ok," Jill murmured and pulled out four dog treats. As the meat flavored biscuits appeared all four dogs sat prim and proper, all motion, save for an inquisitive head tilt, ceasing.

Jill gave each dog one of the treats and then lavished a few moments of attention on them before she un-slung the backpack she wore. As she placed it on the floor and crouched down each dog remained waiting for the treats they expected to be in her pack.

"Sorry to disappoint you, but I'll have to give you more treats later," Jill said to them and pulled her flashlight out the front pocket of her pack. She paused to fend off more licking and then zipped her pack, "Stop now."

The dogs crowded Jill and she sighed, relenting. She stroked their soft grey fur and scratched them each and then kissed their noses. Much like her, they had been locked up while the security team had been at the house. They were used to being free to come and go as they pleased, spending their time between running the estate grounds and lounging around the house. She was angry for them. The four dogs named after Celtic deities had been with the family since Jill was fourteen and they were used to being able to interact with them. Now they were locked in their room and though they had been fed and watered and walked they hadn't gotten their usual exercise.

Jill watched them for a moment, still smiling as they all stood in front of her with tails wagging merrily. The smile slowly crept into a wide grin and she quiet crossed the white tiled floor to the cabinet that the

Quests & Answers

dog's toys were kept in. She peered inside, the dim light from a single night light against the far wall not enough to show her much. Jill glanced at the flashlight she held in one hand and dismissed it. There was no way that a bright light would be ignored by the security teams.

Once again Jill used her phone, partially covering the display with one hand to reduce the light from it as she swept it across one of the shelves. It didn't take long for Jill to find what she was after, a cylindrical container with six brand new yellow tennis balls.

As soon as the container was in her hands the four Irish wolfhounds started for the back door excitedly. Tails that had been lazily wagging were now moving like a berserker's axe smack into the dog next to them as they lined up to rush outside. Jill opened her hand palm down and made a pushing gesture towards the ground and all four dogs immediately dropped into attentive down postures. She closed her hand into a fist, signaling for them to all wait. The four hounds remained motionless, eyes on Jill as she crossed over to where a large bathing tub sat in the middle of a sunken bathing area.

After tucking the canister of tennis balls under one arm Jill grabbed the wide towel rack against the wall and twisted the bar away from her. There was a soft click and the entire tiled section lifted up revealing a stone stairwell heading down into darkness.

Jill heard one of the dogs huff in frustration and turned around, giving them the wait command again before she dropped peered down into the escape tunnel. The tunnel had been there since the original stone keep had been constructed. Their family had kept it through the generations, though until her father had moved in the passage was left spider-filled and dark. Now it had been kept up and ready for use. Jill smiled. Her father Cassidy was a retired SAS officer and very mindful of the family's security. As far back as Jill could remember he had always told the family that because of their means and status they would be targets for criminals. He trained all of his children to spot unusual things like people following them and strange cars. To be ready in case they were ever kidnapped.

Always stay calm. Always have a plan. Always have a way out.

The phrase was a mantra that Jill had learned when she was five. Like most of her father's lessons it had stuck with her. So had the drills the family had run for leaving the house if it were being broken into. All of her sisters had learned of the secret tunnel and all of them knew how to use it and where it ran beneath the property. That meant she only had thirty minutes after the alarm was triggered before someone like her father or Marisa realized she was gone and figured out how she could have left the property. Jill frowned some, and wasn't certain if there was some hidden sensor or indicator that only her father knew about attached to the door, or in the tunnel itself. What Jill was reasonably certain of was that the security teams from Jordan's agency were watching outwards and they could spot her leaving through the tunnel's exit in the woods. She needed a distraction.

Turning, Jill walked across the room towards the backdoor and pulled the container of tennis balls out from under her arm. She popped the black plastic top off and stuffed it in her pocket, looking at the anxiously awaiting dogs, "Wait."

Quests & Answers

Silently, Jill crept over to the window and peered out from behind the side of the burgundy curtain. She was careful not to make the short drape move more than a fractionas she searched for the security teams. Off in the distance about forty meters out she could see a light sweeping about methodically. Jill inhaled and glanced at the dogs. She really hoped that the black clad men were as good as Agent Shaw had said they were. She didn't want any trigger happy trooper getting out of control and shooting the dogs.

Crap.

Worry made Jill hesitate. Her logical mind started running through the scenarios of what could happen if the security teams weren't good, or were just scared of the charging sixty kilo dogs. Then she remembered how scared Marty had been of the men, she could see the fear in his eyes, and the humiliation when his body betrayed him. Seventeen year old hormone-driven rage flattened logic. While logic struggled beneath rage's boot Jill flipped the deadbolt latch for the back door and yanked the handle.

The first tennis ball soared from the open wood door and Jill was almost bowled over by the rush of over two hundred kilos of dog. The animals sped out into the garden and Jill tossed out three more balls which split the dogs in different directions as they each ran to get their own ball. Jill smiled fondly at the animals but only briefly. She turned and hustled into the waiting tunnel, discarding the tennis ball container down at the bottom of the last stair. Using her elbow Jill pressed the switch that closed the hidden door and watched as dim blue lights clicked on along the joins between the ceiling and the walls.

Adrenaline exploded in Jill's veins as she sprinted along the underground passage. She didn't bother to check the corners that had been specifically designed to provide cover in case the tunnel had been compromised. Nor did she pause as she crossed the halfway point where two alcoves held heavy metal storage closets. She had everything she needed in her backpack.

The run across the five acre property seemed to go on and on but soon enough Jill reached a Y where the tunnel split to run east and west. She picked the eastern fork, sliding around the corner as she took it at nearly full speed. The passage made a lazy curve about forty meters ahead and then terminated in a sharp corner with another set of alcoves. Panting, Jill paused to look behind her and listen. The rush of her breath and pounding of her heart obscured any sound. Focusing on breathing in long slow breaths Jill calmed her rushing blood and ravenous lungs. Not fully, but enough for her to listen. When she didn't hear the sound of gunfire, or voices, or footsteps she smiled and did a little shuffling victory dance.

Too bad I won't get to see Jordan's face when she finds out!

Beaming from ear to ear Jill jogged down the passage to where the exit lay. Next to the door there was another alcove with a set of four monitors and a control board. She didn't hesitate as she flipped them all on and looked at the displays. Each monitor was tied to a hidden camera that watched the exit passage and the area surrounding it. The setup always made her think of her dad as James Bond and she grinned as a memory of him showing her how to work them surfaced. There was going to be hell to pay. Jill had no doubt she'd be grounded for a month when her parents got a hold of her. She didn't care. There was no doubt that the security teams and Agent Shaw would suffer far more embarrassment because one of their charges had escaped.

After a minute of watching the monitors Jill shut them all off and walked over to the heavy metal door. It looked like it belonged between bulk heads on a submarine. Dull grey with a shiny silver wheel in the center, it used the same heavy duty rods to keep the door locked. The door's mechanism would lock the door thirty seconds after she shut it and once that was done there was no going back. She wasn't planning to take one of the key fob-like remotes with her; her father had told her numerous times that he would know if they had been used. Even though her escape wasn't going to go unnoticed she didn't want to hasten discovery of her absence.

Jill grabbed the wheel with both hands and turned it to the left. She spun the wheel around three times and the rods smoothly slide from the quarter meter deep holes that allowed them to secure the door to the frame. With both hands still on the wheel Jill hauled the door open and peered out. Jill knew that there was a short flight of stairs in front of her but it was so dark she couldn't even see her own hands. She tucked one hand into her pants pocket and pulled out her flashlight, her thumb depressing the switch.

The small exit passage was filled with crimson light from the small device. The hastily made filter Jill had constructed from red cellophane and a pair of rubber bands worked like a charm. The red light preserved her night vision and more than enough illumination for Jill to see the small trap door at the top of the stairs. It was left mostly as it had been constructed, grey stone blocks set in an earthworks cut. The exterior wasn't sealed like the interior so there was an abundance of moisture and moss on the stone. Jill bounded up the stairs, nearly falling once, and used her free hand to push the trap door up about three centimeters before she slid it backwards. With flashlight in hand she poked her head out of the opening and looked around once more. All she could make out were the bushes that had been strategically planted around the trap door area and the dark boughs of the trees that rose above them. There was a strong earthy smell, a natural smell. The ground around the exit passage was wet from an earlier rain which left the stairs even slipperier at the top, so Jill was careful as she crept higher up the stone steps.

The wood was nearly silent. There was a light wind which made the branches of the trees wave lazily back and forth which created a slight rustling. Satisfied the way was clear, Jill clambered out into the moist air of the English countryside pulling the trap door back in place after her. The door itself was covered with false rocks and moss so that it would blend in with the bushes that surrounded it. Once it was shut Jill crept out from the bushes and made her way through the dark wood. She kept one hand around the lens of the flashlight so she could make an aperture of sorts from her finger which let her control how much light was coming out.

Off in the distance Jill heard the familiar bark of the wolfhounds carried on the night air. She smiled as she thought of the consternation on the security team's faces as the large hounds ran about the garden and property. Her father would soon be out corralling them, if he wasn't already, so she continued towards the edge

Quests & Answers

of the property. It didn't take long to reach it and Jill was confronted with her last hurdle, a three meter tall brick wall.

As she reached the base of it Jill inhaled deeply to try and calm her heart rate again. It didn't work. Swallowing, Jill headed along the wall until she reached a tree that was only about two meters from the wall. She grabbed onto the rough bark with her gloved hands and started up, using the low hanging branches to hoist herself higher. Once she got slightly above the height of the wall Jill scanned what she could see of the forest. Not far away a beam cut through the darkness, the bright white light sweeping through trunks of the trees.

Jill winced as her night vision vanished and blinked furiously to try and clear the stars from her eyes. A second light swept opposite of the first; whoever was carrying them was no more than a couple meters apart. She saw the beams raise up to sweep the branches of a tree and then another.

Shit shit shit, Jill cursed mentally. She had to move or the security team would find her, and there was no way she was going to get caught now.

Logic was still subdued, so it didn't even occur to Jill how easily she could hurt herself. Not once as she shoved off from the trunk of the tree and took two steps along the branch did it register that she could fall and break her neck. Sailing through the air Jill did her best to keep from flailing. She had intended to land on the wall but realized very quickly that she was going over it entirely. Any gloating about her success was cast aside as she came down on the other side of the wall feet first. Thankfully the ground was on the softer side and absorbed much of the impact. Instinctively Jill tucked her legs and let her body roll forward just as she had learned in gymnastics class. Fortunately, she performed better tonight than she had in the short-lived class and managed to roll without breaking anything. After one tumble Jill sprawled out across the ground on her back, her arms and legs almost spread eagle.

The light from the security team's lights swept the branches of the trees. They hadn't seen her but they had heard the branches of the tree when she leapt from it. Without wasting another second, Jill hopped up and started running through the remaining green belt. Once she got to the road Jill looked both ways and pulled her flashlight out again. She pushed the filter off with her thumbs and then clicked it twice to the west. She was greeted by a single, larger, light flashing once.

The growl of a motorcycle's engine starting up reached her ears and Jill started running towards it. The machine, red sport bike, and its single rider came towards her fast. The rider pulled the machine to a stop right in front of Jill and she rushed around to hop up behind the distinctly male form. With one hand the rider flipped up the visor of his red helmet revealing a pair of blue eyes, though the rest of the face was obscured behind the mouth guard of the helmet, "You owe me for this, Jill."

Jill pointed ahead of her and then tightly wrapped her arms around the rider's waist, "I know, Lex. Just go!"

"Alright, alright. Hold on," Lex replied and gunned the bike's engine. The sleek machine sped off down the rural road, its engine purring like a cheetah.

With her arms around Lex's midsection, Jill rested the side of her face against the black and white leather riding jacket he wore. She was surprised how pleasantly solid he felt. Jill's e-mail had promised Lex her sister Deirdre's phone number and fifty pounds for his trouble. The choice may have been the right at the time, however, now Jill pondered just giving the twenty-one year old her own number and the money.

"Where to then?" Lex said in a voice loud enough to be heard over the rushing wind and the snarl of the motorcycle's engine.

"London, but let's swing by a petrol station on the edge of the city, I need to change," Jill replied.

"What's in London?" Lex asked.

Jill's brow furrowed. She hadn't really considered that at all. Her plan only included her getting out and away from the house and not really what to do after her great escape, "Something normal... shopping!"

Lex glanced back at Jill, "Shopping? Nothing's open yet. It's three in the morning."

Jill's stomach rumbled a reminder of her skipped dinner. "And Starbucks. Mmm, yeah, Starbucks," She smiled in anticipation at the thought of a caramel macchiato, extra hot, with a large fluffy blueberry cream cheese muffin. She smiled wide.

With a shake of his head Lex leaned the bike into a corner and raised his voice above the engine, "That's not open yet either. You have no idea where you're going do you?"

"Wherever you are, mate. Let's RIDE!!!" Jill shouted and threw both of her arms in the air above her head. She was free, at least for now and that was good enough.

Without any further conversation Lex cranked his hand back on the throttle. The bike's engine roared filling both he and Jill with the thrill of acceleration.

Jill leaned back into Lex's back and then turned her head so she could look back the way they had come. She checked for signs of pursuit, and seeing none Jill grinned fiercely and flipped her index and middle fingers in the direction of her house. The gesture of defiance made her feel powerful, even if nobody saw it.

In your face, Jordan.

You May Rely On It

By Ren Cummins

Author's note: *Magic eight balls and other delightful forms of otherwise innocent prognostication freak me out a little bit, but not as much as how somberly my subconscious takes it. Buy me Chinese food sometime, and you'll see my almost religious fervor at whatever has been coiled up into my fortune cookie. This started out as a challenge to myself to whip up an homage to the Twilight Zones that fed into my grownup appreciation for my childhood fears. Rod Serling, this one is for you. And, well, to the Shadow who lives under my bed.*

* * * * *

Gary almost laughed when his eyes fixed themselves on the dusty black sphere on the back row of items on the shelf. He'd come in here looking for a nice accent piece for his new cube at work – something with a bit of character to it, maybe something artistic. Maggie had suggested one of those electric meditation fountains, but those just made him need to pee. He'd driven past this old antique shop – why are there never *new* antique shops, he'd mused – various times on his way to or from work, and he simply felt the jones to swing by and check it out today. A sort of celebratory tour in honor of his recent promotion, he decided.

It was a nice – if not mildly overpriced – selection in the musty store. Mostly handmade and well-worn items from the 1920s, some WWII memorabilia and signage, a slightly wobbly coat rack and loads of furniture. He blinked, trying to rationalize the appearance of this silly toy from the 1980s. But his eyes weren't deceiving him – it was a magic eight ball. He reached out and picked it up, blowing the thin layer of dust which had collected on it from presumable months of being overlooked. The faded and handwritten orange sticker listed the price at $1.00. He smiled, shaking it lightly and wondering to himself, *should I buy you, little eight ball*?

He turned it over and nearly dropped it when he read the words float to the surface of the deep indigo liquid: *Yes, you should*.

He looked up, feeling a little strange. He'd never owned one of these back then, but he couldn't remember that having been one of the phrases on the plastic geodesic widgets inside of these toys. "Whoa," he breathed. "That's creepy."

The owner of the store was an older gentleman, likely retired, with a blue shirt and grey slacks which were held up by a pair of dark green suspenders. His thin reading glasses sat further down on his pointy nose than would likely have been helpful, and Gary had the momentary suspicion that he only wore them to add a sense of dignity to his appearance. He was shuffling about near the front window displays with a feather duster, meticulously adding a few million motes to the already cluttered air. The sunlight outside the window seemed almost helpless to penetrate the countless floating specks. The old man looked over at Gary, half-smiled and returned to his task.

Gary was shaking up the ball again, muttering to himself. "Why even bother? The place is just gonna get dusty again in five seconds." He grinned at his pessimistic observation, but stopped instantly when he saw the words floating up on the surface of the eight ball: *I know exactly what you mean.*

He extended his hand, suddenly uneasy with the toy. But before he could replace it, he decided to give it one more test. He closed his eyes, inverting the ball and giving it a gentle shake. *Do you really know what I'm thinking?*

He held his breath, turned it back over and read: *Of course I do.*

He bit his lower lip, furrowed his brow and thought again, giving the ball another spin. "How much do you cost?" he whispered.

When he spun it upright to read the spindle, he gasped. It read: *One Dollar.*

He paid the dollar in cash and left the store.

Gary's apartment was your standard Seattle flat – small bedroom, small living room, small kitchen, with an even smaller bathroom tucked off to the side. He'd been living here for about two years now, and remained among the more affordable parts of his current lifestyle. Though the Capitol Hill area had its random incidents, the local flavor and proximity to his work kept it favorable, and the price had miraculously remained lower than most apartments in the northwest – to say nothing of the downtown housing in general.

They also had a single floor of underground assigned parking – the parking alone was worth its weight in gold. Gary pulled into his space, locked the car and went upstairs, his messenger bag held tightly under his arm.

Up in his apartment, he went about his usual homecoming routine – bag on the couch, keys by the door, wallet on the end table. He microwaved a simple dinner, some flavorless box of something resembling meat with vegetables and some sort of opaque sauce. The light on the answering machine was flashing, but for some reasons he didn't feel like checking it. His eyes returned to the bag each time he walked back through the living room, and, after a few minutes, he finally settled down on the couch next to it. He unsnapped the latch and drew out the black plastic ball.

Holding it in his left hand, he used his thumbnail to scrape off the price sticker. "I'll say one thing for you, you really don't look like an unusual toy," he muttered. "Just like any other random magic eight ball."

He flipped it over, and read the words as they floated to the top.

Ask a question.

Chuckling, he turned it back over, and asked, "What makes you so special?"

The ball then read: *I always tell the truth.*

"Always?"

You may rely on it.

"Good touch," Gary laughed. "But it's kind of... weird. You don't mind if I put you to the test or something?"

It's up to you.

"Okay, then...hmmm..." Gary looked around the room, finally grabbing the remote and turning on the TV. CNN faded into life, the talking head there sharing the screen with a graphic of a meteor or something, and talking about 'most favorable conditions' or whatnot. "What's on TV right now?" he asked the ball.

The News, the ball responded.

"Whoa. Cool." Gary flipped a few channels, stopping on a football game: Patriots versus the Oilers. The Pats were up by three with only seconds remaining. "Who's winning?"

The Oilers.

Gary's smile froze. He looked from the ball to the screen a couple times. "Okay, well, you're wrong. That's, just... weird."

Wait for it.

At that moment, there was a commotion on the screen. Gary looked up to see one of the Oilers' defensive lineman pick up a fumble and run the ball all the way to their end zone, a few seconds after the time ran out. Final score now showed the Oilers winning by three points.

"Oh my god. That's amazing! How'd you do that?"

Hello. Magic Eight Ball.

"But seriously, that's really cool. Um… what should I do now?" he asked, unable to think of anything at the moment.

Take a shower.

"What? Why?"

You stink.

"Nice. I meant, was there some reason in particular?"

Big day tomorrow.

"What kind of 'big day'? Am I gonna win the lottery?"

You don't play the lottery.

"Well, if I was going to *win*, I'd play," Gary explained. "Though I suppose that kind of defeats the purpose of gambling, doesn't it?"

Good answer.

"So you're not going to tell me what's going to happen, besides telling me it's a big day?"

Bingo.

Gary frowned. "I can't even play 'hot or cold' or something?"

Quit stalling.

"Geez. For a plastic oracle, you're pretty pushy."

You should meet my sister.

He laughed, delicately set the ball back on the table and went off to the bathroom. Whatever this "big day" was all about, it couldn't hurt to be prepared.

Morning. 5:30 am. Gary turned off the alarm and practically jumped out of bed. Dressed and cleaned up in record time, he walked into the living room and went straight to the magic eight ball. He'd picked it up before he'd even realized he didn't know what to ask. He grimaced a moment, then simply turned the ball over.

You're going to be late.

He looked at the clock, which showed ten minutes before 6. Normally, he ran out the door around 6:10, and still got to work on time. "You're off your mind, man. I'm totally early." His mind flashed back to the last-second, come-from-behind win in the football game. Frowning, he turned the ball over. "Why am I going to be late?"

You'll miss the bus.

"Whatever you say," he laughed. He placed the ball in his messenger bag and picked up the ring of keys by the door. "It's called owning a car, mister Wizard."

He locked up behind himself, took the elevator down to the parking level of his building, and stood for five minutes in front of his empty parking space.

"You could've told me the car was stolen," he muttered. "In fact, you could've warned me that the car was *going* to be stolen." He looked down his shoulder at the bag. "No, I can already bet what you're going to say. '*You didn't ask.*'"

Snapping his fingers, he unzipped the bag and pulled out the ball. "Where's my car?"

It's called car theft.

"Smart ass. Now what?"

You'll miss the bus.

He could already hear the bus arriving at the corner as he ran from the parking lot entrance. He stopped at the corner, bent over with his hands on his knees, panting heavily. He didn't waste time with the ball; most likely, it already knew what he was thinking.

He finally got to work fifteen minutes late, tossed his messenger bag on the desk and sat at his computer. For having a miraculous prognosticating ball, his day was off to a fairly craptacular beginning. Shaking his head, he pulled up his email – the most recent one was from his girlfriend, Maggie.

Didn't hear from you last night. Is everything okay? Bad news, I can't make it to dinner today, I got called into an emergency office planning meeting. Call me later?

– Mags

He sighed. They'd been dating on and off for a couple years now, and with their time being dedicated so much of late to their respective jobs, they didn't see each other very much at all. He'd half thought the ball's promise of today being a "big day" might even be a hint at some new direction in their relationship. His head rested down on his desktop. This day was *not* going well.

"You okay, Gary?"

He sat up. It was Amy, from two cubes down. They'd engaged in casual "office flirting" for the past few months, ever since she'd broken up with her boyfriend. She was attractive, but he hadn't really given it any serious thought. But now… He smiled. "Yeah, just a little winded. Someone stole my car and I missed the bus and…" he chuckled. "But I'm here, so that's something."

"I'm going downstairs for a coffee. Want to come with?"

He took a slow breath. "Nnnoooo, I think I better get to work, I'm already late." He added, after a moment of mentally kicking himself, "but thanks. Maybe next time?"

She nodded, smiling. She had a nice smile. "Okay. Be right back, then."

He sat back in his seat, shaking his head. His hand reached into his bag, pulled out the 8 ball. "Moron or hero?" he asked, mostly to himself.

Moron.

"We're gonna talk about my car when I get back," he muttered, putting the ball down and jumping up. He called out after Amy, catching up to her as she held the elevator door for him. She did have a very nice smile.

The rest of day was lively. He and Amy chatted over instant messenger, and it was actually enjoyable – any guilt he might have otherwise felt was fading fast under the barrage of Amy's obvious interest.

Before he knew it, it was getting close to lunchtime. He looked from his email window to his instant message window and, from there, to the magic eight ball. He found himself hoping for a specific answer to his unspoken question before he even touched the ball.

Ask Amy.

He had a small thrill of excitement when she messaged him "yes", even though the ball had already told him she'd accept.

They decided to go to a nearby diner – it was pleasant and cozy, and the food wasn't bad. They took a booth near the window and made small talk. Things went nicely – the gentle tingle of potential attraction was intoxicating, and a good enhancement to the meal.

About five minutes before the check arrived, Gary got that sinking feeling – the strange "someone is looking at me" vibe, the herald of doom, if ever it had a name. He looked out the window to see Maggie and two of her friends standing, staring at him. He couldn't tell if Maggie was about to cry or throw one of her friends through the window at him.

Needless to say, the lunch ended poorly. He'd run after Maggie and tried to talk to her, but her friends ran interference until one of the chefs from the restaurant caught up with him and threatened to call the police on Gary for running out on the bill. In the commotion, Maggie and friends made their escape. Gary went with the chef back to the restaurant in time for Amy to slap him across the face and leave. He settled the bill and slowly made his way back to work.

His manager met him on his way back to his desk, and they had a brief conversation regarding interoffice relationships and his repeated tardiness. He slumped into his chair and glared at the magic eight ball. Snapping it up from the desk, he tried to calm himself.

It's not my fault.

"What do you mean it's not your fault?" he whispered. "You said to ask Amy!"

That's right.

"But it ruined everything! Now she hates me, Maggie hates me, and my job's in danger!"

That's also right.

"Wait…" he frowned, "are you just trying to ruin my life, or is this one of those things where you trim out all the bad things so that I get something good?"

Trust me.

Gary sighed. "Well, we still need to figure out where my car is."

The widget seemed to take its time rising to the surface. *Don't worry about it.*

His eyes narrowed and a long breath made its way from his nostrils. "Easy for you to say, all you have to do is tell the future." If the ball answered him, he didn't waste any time reading it. He had four more hours on the clock to try and salvage his job, and would probably need every available second of it.

At some point after 5:30, he capped off a pretty horrible day with some reasonably impressive reports, and watched his manager reluctantly concede that Gary'd still have a future with the company, which, at this point, Gary was prepared to accept as a victory. Amy had already left, so thankfully he didn't have to avoid eye contact on his way to the elevator.

He was already halfway across the parking lot before he remembered that his car had been stolen, and, having no better ideas, sat down on the parking block and pulled out the magic eight ball. It was a cloudy evening, unusually warm with the sky the gentle orange of sunset. He looked across the street at a convenience store. The word "Lotto" blazed at him, its undeniable temptation feeding into his frustration.

"Should I start playing the lottery?" he asked. A woman was leaving the store at that moment, a small nylon bag of groceries in her hand.

Don't bother.

"What, you're not going to help me win quick cash? Some help you are. Is there some rule or something that won't let you help me get rich?"

That's not it.

"Then why?" The woman had turned the corner, leaving Gary alone with his increasing frustration.

She has the winning ticket.

Gary closed his eyes. He could probably hit the far wall from here with this stupid ball.

Yes, you probably could.

The widget rolled of its own accord, changing to read: *But please don't.*

"Give me a good reason why I shouldn't! My whole life is ruined – I've lost my car, my girlfriend, and almost lost my job, all from listening to you."

It's for the best.

Gary sighed. "Yeah, and now you're gonna tell me how I'm going to do something really big in the future that will save the world or something, and it's all because of all the crap you've helped happen now."

No. Not at all.

"Not really helping your case, man."

Your car was a piece of crap.

"Dude. Totally uncalled for."

It was.

Gary sighed. It was a piece of crap. It was paid off, but it was starting to nickel and dime him. Still, it was paid off and that meant something.

"Fine, I'll agree with that, but Maggie?"

You didn't love her.

Gary stopped as he was about to argue with the ball. As much as he hated to admit it, he didn't really love her. They'd been together for a long time, but he really didn't see the relationship going anywhere. Maybe it was for the best that they broke up and she found someone else who really cared for her like she deserved.

Exactly.

"Okay, fine. So you haven't totally ruined my life, then. But at least she'd be able to come give me a ride home."

Also true.

"So, see? That would've been a good thing, then."

Not for her.

He shook his head. "Thanks, that's really nice. I get that she deserves better, but it's not like giving me a ride home would've killed her."

Funny you should say that.

Gary read this latest response twice. "What do you mean?"

Nothing. Don't worry about it.

"Oh no, you don't. You meant something." He shook the ball. "You said you always tell the truth. What did you mean by that?"

The little widget seemed to take its time in floating to the surface. When it finally slid into place against the clear plastic, Gary nearly dropped the ball.

You're going to die.

Gary's throat nearly closed. "Wha- what? When? How?"

Now.

He blinked at the unexpected revelation. "No way. You've got to be joking or...something. Right?"

I'm sorry.

"But - - -but how?" The words "I'm sorry" repeated on the ball. Gary shook it again, harder. "Tell me!"

It doesn't matter.

"It matters to me!"

You can't avoid it.

"At least tell me! I can try to... I don't know, change it, or something!"

No, you can't.

"Don't you tell me that!" he screamed. He stood up, oblivious to the people pausing briefly in passing to stare at the man's apparent argument with a small black plastic sphere.

"I've watched those movies, there's always a way to change the future or something!"

I only tell the truth.

Gary looked into the ball. It all seemed darker, somehow, like all the light had gone out of the world. He felt defeated, exhausted. The air tasted like ash in his mouth, the air felt dry and bitter. His eyes welled up, and he looked back at the crystal ball in his hands.

Don't look up, it read.

He didn't.

Li Bai

By Quiana Kirkland

L i Bai awoke with his face pressed against the window, a small trickle of saliva making a sticky stream down the soft terrain of his cheek. He cracked one eye open and high pitched squeals pierced the air. He was snout to snout with two small freckled faces. Slowly he turned his back to the naked cubs, the flashes of many cameras creating a strobe-like affect, his iconic black and white fur flickering like old film beyond the smudged glass. This magic reversal, life imitating cinema, was lost on Li Bai.

For months Li Bai had been depressed, but nobody had noticed. Every day Li Bai would wake up and do everything he was supposed to do. He'd eat his greens, wash his face, and clean his claws. Until one morning when Li Bai sat slowly eating his rations of bamboo, vacantly crunching the carefully hidden vitamins. As he stared out the window to where the naked bears crowded, his chewing came to a sudden stop. His furry chin hung slack with the realization that all he had to show for his years of good behavior was a mammoth collection of fibrous dumps.

"What does it mean?" thought Li Bai, as he looked back and forth from the blurry windows to the chopped bamboo in his paws. *"Why do I eat this bamboo and where does it come from?"* The first question opened the way for others, springing forth like water from a fine leak in a dam. Answerless questions spurting into the air and landing on the floor of his home, making a mess of things. *Why am I here? Why do they watch me? What is on the other side of that window?* The naked bears jumped with surprise as Li Bai bounded to his feet and began pacing the perimeter of his home, inspecting everything for a clue, a reason, meaning. As though one piece of straw or dried up leaf could patch up the hole in his understanding and cure his restless mind.

Li Bai's minders thought that this restlessness was a sign of new found maturity. *"Perhaps it was time to mate Li Bai?"* they wondered aloud to each other. After lengthy negotiations with another facility they pushed a she-bear into his enclosure. She was gentle and beautiful; her fur true white, like soft clouds in a dark night sky. Li Bai and the new bear ate bamboo as the sunset lit their soft white fur gold, red, and orange. Li Bai fell asleep. The she-bear went home and cried wondering if she had gotten fat.

The minders were puzzled. They took Li Bai from his enclosure and brought him to a shiny room with a bright white sun. They poked him and prodded him and put him into a deep sleep even as he struggled to bite and tear their naked pink skin.

He woke up at home groggy and bruised. He was angry. Li Bai had not been angry before. It was new and fiery. And even though it scared him, he liked being this new angry bear. Li Bai felt strong.

He ate his bamboo with a new ferocity; using his teeth, carnivore's teeth, to shred the leaves from the stalk. And as happens when one is angry and not paying attention, Li Bai bit his thumb. It hurt... a lot. Li Bai brought his thumb up in front of his eyes and inspected it. There was a collective gasp from the naked bears. Their cameras clicked furiously. He put his paw down, surprised. The clicking stopped. He raised it again, his thumb pointing up into the air. The naked bears excitedly pointed their thumbs towards the sky too. Li Bai took great joy in seeing how excited he'd made the naked bears. That night when they brought him less than fresh bamboo he did not eat it. The next day they brought him honey treats and Li Bai thrust his sticky thumb in the air. They put their thumbs up too.

Li Bai had communicated with the naked bears. And though this didn't solve the greater questions of why the bamboo existed and why Li Bai was there to eat it, Li Bai began to get nice and fat using his new power. Soon the questions-leak which had driven Li Bai to such distraction was patched with honey and toys.

Every day more and more naked bears and minders came to view him and Li Bai grew proud. He would swagger across the straw laden concrete on feet like fuzzy novelty slippers, then roll onto his back and expose his vast belly to the adoring crowds, basking in the flashing lights as he thrust his thumb into the air. He drank their attention in lustily, knowing he deserved all of it and more. Though he did not know it, Li Bai had created God in his own image. Exalted, he lolled about like a drunk, intoxicated by the power of an idolized deity.

A bear thinking only of visceral satisfaction, Li Bai lived on honey cakes alone. One day the small barred door opened and the she-bear reluctantly shuffled out. This time Li Bai was intrigued, but while they were rolling about in his cottony bed of straw she let out a noise which was somewhere between a squeak and an 'ouf.' With difficulty Li Bai raised himself and the she-bear stumbled towards the door and into the waiting arms of the minders. Li Bai was very annoyed by all the fuss.

The next morning there were no honey cakes, just a pile of bamboo. *"No thumbs up today,"* thought Li Bai, turning his back on the window and going to sleep in a warm patch of sunlight, wondering what the She Bear was doing. Wondering if she was thinking of him. When Li Bai awoke the moon was shinning dully upon the same stale pile of bamboo. Having no choice and a ravenous appetite, Li Bai grabbed the bamboo and wolfed it down in a darkened corner of his home. He would eat it, but they would have no satisfaction from him.

Days came and went and Li Bai was given only bamboo- and not a lot of it. With every small meal his hunger and frustration festered and swelled. Soon Li Bai was quite slender by panda standards. But they did not bring the She Bear back. Li Bai sat in his loneliness like a cold bath. Bitter and childish, he would climb to the top of his giant concrete stump and stare moodily out, filled again with the same old questions.

One morning, having consumed his meager meal, he looked over his wall and saw someone… different.

This stranger looked roughly like Li Bai in shape, but was more delicate than Li Bai, with soft brown fur with a golden yellow chest. Li Bai raised his thumb into the air and waved it frantically. The other bear cocked his head at Li Bai and climbed back down his own stump rapidly. Li Bai watched the other side of the wall all day, but at last climbed down having seen nothing more of the stranger.

Li Bai could not sleep that night. He rolled this way and that restlessly, new scents in the breeze jerking him awake to hear the normal sounds of the night. Finally, Li Bai gave up the idea of sleep and again climbed the giant stump. And there right across from him was the same bear paw raised in greeting. Li Bai waved, the black shag of his arm moving in counterpoint to his paw like a dark undulating wave. The other bear pointed to the corner between their homes. Li Bai slid down the rough trunk and ran to a small grate in the thick grey wall. Three sets of golden eyes shone in the dull light, like coins deep under water. Li Bai pushed his snout into the space between the bars and inhaled deeply, touching the other bears' noses in turn, black nose to brown. He smelled musky fur and something sweet.

"Hello, Brother, how good it is to meet you," said the largest of the three. Li Bai's joy filled him all the way to his eyes, before, stinging, it escaped in the form of hot tears. "My name is Li Bai," croaked a voice so little-used that the sound of it surprised Li Bai himself. "I am not alone," Li Bai whispered. The largest bear grabbed his paw through the tightly fitted bars, "You never were, for God was with you."

Li Bai began to meet the sun bears every night. The night after they met Li Bai asked about what they meant by God. The sun bears were shocked to find out that Li Bai had never heard of Him, or The Jungle. "He grows the bamboo," they told Li Bai gesturing from the sky to the ground. "God makes bamboo?" Li Bai asked with wonder, "I have always wondered that." "He also makes the water," the smallest bear chimed in, his grin wide. Li Bai immediately responded, "Why?" "For us to drink!" The sun bears all laughed and assured Li Bai that they had all the answers.

When Li Bai asked why they lived in these enclosures, the sun bears told him that they lived in a temple. They explained that they were representatives of God. This is why the things they needed appeared; Li Bai learned that these are called blessings. Li Bai was the perfect vessel, entirely empty, aching to be filled. And the sun bears were sincerely excited to have someone to take in all their wisdom. It pleased them to help a poor soul like Li Bai find meaning and they congratulated themselves for it heartily.

Li Bai had finally gotten everything he'd wished for and more than he'd known to want. Flush with companionship and answers, his smile burst from his face so determinedly that his cheeks were sore. It is at this time of contentment, of course, that Li Bai learned to want more.

It was their stories about The Jungle which filled Li Bai with an urgent longing that eventually matched his former desires. "The Jungle," the sun bears explained, waving their furry arms about, "is like this place, but with greens on the floor and bamboo on the ceiling. All for the taking." The luxury in which they lived now was nothing, the sun bears exhorted, compared to The

Jungle. The sun bears were so wise that they had answers even to questions Li Bai had never considered. They knew how to get to the Jungle, and wanted Li Bai to come with them.

The sun bears told him that if did what they told him, he could come with them from the temple to The Jungle when they left. The bears told him to observe them and live as they lived, so Li Bai began paying close attention to the sun bear's daily activities. They bowed to the sky and raced about hunting for pieces of fruit, gifts from their God. They would gobble the soft fruit pulp and then roll around in the rinds. In the afternoons they would meditate in the sunshine, perfectly motionless. Li Bai began to bow to the sky too, but no matter how hard he looked, no sacred snacks appeared, and he was jealous and ashamed of his jealousy. Li Bai knew he was doing it wrong, but didn't know how to tell the sun bears.

Every evening after the sun had set, the sun bears would come to Li Bai and teach him the ways of their God and the righteous path to The Jungle. Sometimes they told him the stories they heard as young bears and Li Bai learned all about kings, monsters, and princesses- in addition to what to eat and how to pray. Li Bai devoured their stories, gulping them down hungrily to fill the emptiness of his life with rules and reason.

But most of all Li Bai was taught all that he had done wrong. Wanting things. Then getting them and wanting more. Or not getting them and being sad. Eating too much. Asking for too much. And of course, the lust. Always the impurity of his thoughts. Though slow to start, Li Bai's continued curiosity about the possibilities presented by the She Bear were nearly impossible to squelch. So many nights Li Bai lay awake trying to think only of God. *Don't think about shining fur, dulcet voices, bright eyes, or soft pink lips. Don't think about bamboo. Don't think. Please!* Li Bai would squeeze his eyes tightly and recite words taught to him by the sun bears, his hands firmly planted on his face.

Everything Li Bai desired was wrong. As he would meditate, his innumerable sins would stretch thin and tight along the horizon in a fine, but infinitely long line. Soon his worries about sinning were far more numerous than the number of questions that had so troubled him to begin with.

Li Bai awoke earlier and earlier to atone for his ever increasing iniquities; and, one morning as the sun just began pinking the sky, he bent into position high atop his stump. As he sat a soft skritching came from the sun bear's home. He smiled realizing that they would see him up and meditating before them and smiled. Then added pridefullness to his list. He cracked open one eye and in the dim light Li Bai could just make out two naked bears in the sun bear's home. Squinting, Li Bai saw them carefully hiding chunks of cut fruit all around. He was so surprised he nearly fell from his stump. *What could this mean? If they bring the fruit, how do we know it is from God? If fruit grows in The Jungle, and the naked bears give us fruit, do they come from The Jungle? Are they gods?* Li Bai was deeply confused, and just as before the little trickle of questions became a torrent.

That evening when the bears sat crowded around the grate Li Bai asked them about what he had seen. "There is only one God, Li Bai," the sun bears told him eyeing, him suspiciously. The oldest of the sun bears reached out for Li Bai through the grate, "God works through everything, especially the naked bears. The entire universe and all in it are manipulated in the pinks of His paws. You must have faith that everything we say is true. This is what faith means. You must be trusting as a cub, believing that which cannot be proven, to go to The Jungle."

Li Bai had numerous follow up questions about God growing strong within his mind like stubborn weeds, winding so deep that he could not extricate their strangling roots on his own. But the sun bears became frustrated with Li Bai's impertinent questions, hurt that he was so disbelieving. They urged him to have faith and spend more time in meditation.

Li Bai prayed constantly; yet, he felt no peace, received no reward. Still, questions lingered in the back of his mind, waiting to explode, in spite of his best efforts to have faith. Li Bai wondered if faith meant the same thing to the sun bears as it did to him. They had taught him to think and told him to question, but now they wanted him to stop. He worried that his only company would abandon him. That he would never make it to The Jungle. Within him a cold tightness burned, and while he pushed it down, Li Bai began to worry that he never believed in The Jungle, because it and God never existed at all.

When darkness fell the next night only one sun bear arrived to speak with Li Bai, and Li Bai's sore feelings were again injured. *They're already leaving me,* he thought, feeling that deep tightness in his chest. The sun bear glanced around nervously and leaned close, "I know you've been speaking with him, the black bear," he said, ignoring Li Bai's questioning expression and rushing to continue hissing, "but Li Bai, listen," he gestured to a neighboring wall, "the other bear, his kind, they will only bring you down." Li Bai barely heard the sun bear's warning over the thoughts buzzing around in his head.

Li Bai was curious about the other bear and hovered for days by the grill in what he hoped was their shared wall. Eventually a giant black snout and coal-dark eye appeared behind the cold metal lattice. As they crouched in the corner Black Bear told Li Bai his secrets. Black Bear had not been raised in the "temple" or anyplace like it. He laughed at Li Bai's belief in God, telling him that they were not priests, but prisoners. Li Bai did not believe him, but said nothing. Black Bear told Li Bai that they lived in a "zoo," a prison, where naked bears came to spy on other bears. He looked around himself as though worried that someone would hear as he explained that just as inside the zoo, the naked bears ruled the outside world. He looked at Li Bai through the bars and whispered, "*They leave food in boxes outside their dens and kidnap any bear who goes near it. I knew better, but I was starving. One moment I was eating and the next I was here.... I think they are studying us. We've got to get escape.*"

There was a subtle shift in mood and Li Bai's expression of rapt interest hiccupped briefly ahead of a lengthy silence. Li Bai did not know what to say about this, as it was the exact opposite of everything he'd been taught, everything he'd believed. And yet within him that fear that all he'd learned was a lie ached. It seemed preposterous that the minders slavishly serve them if they were prisoners. Why bring him honey cakes and she-bears? And yet Black Bear had seen it with his own eyes and was terrified. Li Bai politely made his excuses and returned to his straw bed, his mind swimming with foreign gods and shanghais.

He did not sleep that night as he ruminated on what he'd been told. In the following days he worried on the issues until he realized that regardless of who was right black bear or sun bear, he could not be happy. He vacillated between believing that The Jungle was real and he'd never get there and feeling that The Jungle never existed to begin with. Li Bai lay alone by his food bowl and grew bitter. He could no longer meditate, becoming instantly furious at the slightest noise or movement. Black Bear would wake up and sharpen his claws, scratching over and over again against the cement, preparing his escape. Day in and day out he scratched, the noise grating through Li Bai's mind, sending shivers down his back. Li Bai thought that Black Bear was crazy, feared that maybe they were all crazy and that is why they were there.

Even the joyful prayers and worship from his godly neighbors disgusted him and filled him with a sourness that bubbled up from deep within. There are no gods, no Jungle; nothing was there that you couldn't touch right now. Li Bai knew the sun bears were fools and he despised them. The sound of their bowings and scrapings jangled together with the naked bears' camera clicks, and Black Bear's paranoid scratching to drum the beat of Li Bai's discontent; a veritable symphony of loathing.

Some days Li Bai only believed in the paw in front of his face and other days he wondered if it was all someone else's dream and none of them existed at all.

Not knowing what to do with Li Bai in this manic state, the minders brought back the she-bear. She followed him around as he tried to avoid her dull presence. Ever in his way, deaf and dumb, he would try to speak to her but all she knew was bamboo and bamboo made her happy.

That night Li Bai sat with his back to the she-bear. She extended her paw to him and touched his shoulder. He felt nothing, cold and hollow on the inside like the bars on the walls. From the silence came the heavy sounds of breathing. Li Bai realized that the minders were still there, watching them. This invasion of his privacy, it was all her fault. Before she came along, the minders would at least leave him alone during the night. Li Bai shook with barely restrained anger. In the back of his home he heard rolling and a sudden high pitch buzz. He turned and squinted into the bright light which expanded from a pinpoint to a rectangle on a large box. The minders retreated and suddenly the air was filled with moans of passion. On the device two pandas were being… intimate.

Li Bai sat in horror. "*How dare they bring filth into my home,*" he thought immediately of The Jungle. The she-bear leaned forward again to stroke his face and he slapped her. She cried out and the minders rushed in as Li Bai bellowed, turning on her again. She scrabbled backwards and he advanced on her. Li Bai swung at her and she rolled head over foot with a squeal. He ran forward, ignoring the minders' attempts to snag him and beat her with balled up paws, tears flying from his eyes.

The minders pulled him off the she bear, her blood soaking slowly across her fur. In the darkness she looked just like Black Bear to him. He snapped and clawed at the terrified minders until he felt the slightest pinch on his back. As Li Bai slid from consciousness, he realized that he wasn't a god, priest, or king. At last, he understood that he was simply an animal; a monster from a children's story.

Thunder and Three

By Garth Reasby

T he trees around the small band felt as if they were slowly closing in around them. Tall and dark with wood knotted by age and the cancerous intent of wicked men, the ancient oaks rose above them, arching up and then drooping down as if reaching towards the purifying light of the sun was more than they could bear. There was little sound here in the dark wood, just the occasional sound of armor and equipment rustling against itself and the body that bore it.

The thick canopy so very high in the air suffocated the sounds of wind, and no animal seemed willing to dare the dark wood. No bird, no rabbit, not even the large wolves that were so commonly seen stalking the forested pathways of other sections of the Great Wood itself.

There was very little discussion amongst the four warriors, every sense was focused on the wood around them, though they could only make out the sounds that they brought into this place. Only see the effects of their passage. A footstep in graying moss. The echo of a well worn shield bumping the hilt of a blade or the haft of a spear.

"Silence..." Intoned the lead warrior, his normally rich voice usually full of warmth and passion was but a harsh whisper that seemed far louder than it should. His cobalt gaze turned to his three companions, his angled features half hidden by the shadow caused by his long blonde locks. He adjusted his grip on the hammer he carried, the short but stout weapon perfect for laying an enemy low in close quarters.

"Every movement sounds as if we are carrying pots and pans from the kitchen. See to your equipment."

"Speak not of kitchens and pots and pans. All I can think of is a warm leg of meat and a large mug of mead. My stomach will protest more loudly than the kit of an army if we don't find game soon." The largest of the four replied. His size was not in just height, but weight. He had the girth of a noble lord long in the tooth with a well stocked larder, yet he bore it well and moved as nimbly as the rest. Though he stood a full head taller than the blonde warrior that lead them, even he felt small amongst the towering black oaks. The man who was both tall and wide shook his head in response to how loud his own voice seemed to be here, even the sound of his long fiery red beard brushing across his breastplate seemed to sound like steel scraping stone.

"I would eat nothing from this foul wood. Not rabbit, nor deer, nor even a berry if any of such existed here. Even you, my powerful friend, should rely on what you have stocked in your manly girth lest you become as tainted as this black place." The warrior who preferred to dress in green leathers replied. He reached up to stroke his neatly trimmed blonde goatee before tightening the rust colored sword belt he wore across his body. He was the leanest of the four, and the

Quests & Answers

shortest, though still tall by most men's standards. He took much pride in his appearance and displayed such as he pulled the hem of his leather tunic straight.

"Well spoken and true. This place is dark, and fell and we would be considered wise if we tarried not here." Intoned the last, his whispering voice the only of the four that didn't sound as if it was shouting in the unnatural silence of the wood. He too tightened the belts he wore, and ensured that his chain hauberk was secured against the black leathers he wore. His fierce gaze was cast in the direction of his companions, noting that moment of frustration from the largest of them as well as the preening of the shortest. His own movements were efficient and silent as he ensured his equipment was tied securely in place.

The leader once more turned to look at the four men, his stormy gaze focusing on each of their faces as he took in their measure. Nodding in satisfaction, he adjusted his winged helmet and turned to march deeper into the ancient black wood,

"Aye this place is fell but our quarry and quest lie at its heart. Now silence, lest we be undone by witty banter that is best saved for the mead hall."

That earned a nod of acknowledgement from the three warriors and without further comment they returned to their march, the sounds of their passage lessened but still audible to the one that watched them from the shadowy embrace of an ancient oak's branches.

The one, the lurker, smiled a smile that was wide and laden with darkness. It was darker than the wood though not so dark as the soul of she who wore it. With charms and enchantment wrapped around her slender form like a warm winter's cloak she followed the four. She knew well how to remain silent in a wood that would betray the presence of those who tread its' paths.

Not a trace of sound was made by her steps. No click of boot heel on stone. No sound of breath exhaled. No rustle of branch on cloak. Even desiccated leaves, dry and crisp, remained silent as if unwilling to betray her step. Shrouded in darkness she made her way

Darkness held her hand and she held its'. Her golden tresses hidden in the shade of darkness' will, bound to her as it was by spell and craft. So thusly, she followed the Thunder and Three, quietly stalking the path that they trod. Her determination no less than theirs for she knew that the reward she sought was also on this path that they all walked.

Unlike the four she felt not the touch of hunger. She knew well the dark forest's ways and came armed with enchantments instead of blades. No, she knew well the dark forest's ways. The lures it would use to trap fools within its' winding paths.

Any beast's flesh that crossed the lips would corrupt and twist until only a beast remained. Many fools had eaten well in the forest so it was rife with beasts. Yet, as darkness often did, they fed on themselves in seasons where fools were rare. The strongest of the beasts grew stronger and more fell with each taste of its' kin's flesh. Darkness granted it yet more strength though such a strength became its' burden. For every kin eaten, or every fool devoured, it hungered even more.

She who walked in darkness' embrace smiled and watched the four continue their march deeper into the wood.

London 1865

By H. L. Reasby

Author's Note: As an author, the Victorian period is an incredibly intriguing timeframe. It sits on a wonderful cusp between the religious and the scientific, and is a time when those two juggernauts are often butting heads. In particular, the science of investigation and law enforcement underwent many changes. This story was very much inspired by the Robert Downey Jr. version of Sherlock Holmes.

* * * * *

Rounding the corner to hurry to her master's townhouse, Lila got no more than four steps down the street before the peace of the upscale neighborhood was shattered. The blast sent horses scattering, their drovers trying desperately to regain control as carts careened behind them. Screams of pain and terror pierced the air as shrapnel ripped through bystanders. The force of the blast literally lifted Lila off her feet and sent her tumbling backward, her basket shattering as she hit the ground, the flowers it contained shredding and sending petals flying. Dazed and shell-shocked, she didn't even register the pain from her ruptured eardrums or the trickles of blood seeping from her ears. Slowly, as though moving through molasses, Lila reached for the flowers, trying to gather them back to her.

Oh, the mistress will be so angry. The thought flitted through Lila's mind, drifting like the lilac petals on the explosion's pressure wave.

She couldn't hear the clatter of debris falling from the sky as the blast subsided into fire, but moments later, strong hands gripped her under the arms and lifted her from the ground. Even in Lila's dazed state, she recognized the face of Gerard Trask who lived several houses down and across the street from the family she worked for.

Lila's mistress and her lady friends played at being scandalized that a mere constable lived in their strictly upper-crust neighborhood, but even as they complained, their tones turned quietly salacious as they discussed him. Among the servants, they were more frank about such things and Lila knew she was far from the only one who harbored a crush on him. With his tall, muscular build, darker-toned skin, and consistently shorn hair, he radiated an intensity that was simultaneously magnetic and intimidating.

Cradled in Trask's strong arms, Lila relished the moment, breathing in the smell of his aftershave to share with her friends later. The term shock wasn't one she associated with the state she was in. For the moment, she felt warm and safe and unconcerned about the explosion that had rocked the quiet street.

Lila smiled as she saw another familiar face, Molly, the constable's housekeeper. The petite redhead was on the steps of Trask's townhouse, holding a large basket of bandages and a jug of water. She moved forward to help Trask settle Lila onto the steps of the house. As

Molly worked on cleaning Lila up, Trask turned and ran back toward the epicenter to bring more people out of harm's way.

Hours later, former constable Gerard Trask stood on the steps, watching the cleanup and investigation of the explosion's cause. At that moment, the brick of his residence behind him was more expressive than Trask's face and everyone gave him a wide berth. He'd sent Molly off to hospital with Lila and the other injured, empowering her to make arrangements for payment for their care in his name if they had no one else to help.

The blast had leveled nearly the entire townhouse and had caused severe damage to the houses on either side of it. Broken masonry, splintered wood, shattered glass, and powdered plaster littered the street which had been closed off to traffic. Although the surrounding area had, in theory, been evacuated until the gas flow could be stopped, that didn't stop a large crowd of the concerned and the curious from gathering. Their presence forced the investigating officers to spend just as much time keeping civilians out from underfoot as they did trying to figure out what had happened.

A shift of the crowd's movements opened a space suddenly and emotion became visible as Trask's face darkened. It was like a vicious storm rolling in off the ocean, frightening and implacable in its fury.

A child's toy lay in the center of the street. The plush honey-colored fur of the stuffed rabbit was pristine on the left side, but the right had been charred and the ear on that side had been burned away entirely. A muscle jumped in Trask's jaw as he saw the stretchers start to come out; four that were clearly adults and three small ones that were, without doubt, not.

Turning, he walked up the steps and went inside, the door closing quietly behind him.

Molly sighed as she picked up the oiled leather overcoat that had been discarded by the door. "Shudder to think what this place would look like if I weren't about to pick up," she grumbled to herself as she opened the coat closet and hung the garment properly.

Small and willowy in build with lush red hair that fell in curls to the small of her back when unbound, Molly had recently had her twentieth birthday, though there were times she felt much older than her years. The last few years since Trask had taken her in, years without privation, fear or abuse, had erased most outward signs of her less-than-wholesome early life. Thanks to tutors and decent clothing, Molly could now speak to some members of the upper-class without being immediately looked on as a low-brow gutter-snipe.

The flat was quite large for Trask to have afforded on a constable's salary, but given his education and his well-spoken manner, Molly assumed that there must have been money in his family and which he had inherited. She picked up her satchel again and glanced at the fine silver dish on the table inside the door. She noted that the few calling cards that she had collected and left there for him had been removed.

The décor of the flat was unrelentingly masculine, the woods and fabrics tending to be dark and heavy, the sparse furnishings more utilitarian than stylish. There were few paintings, mostly landscapes, and none of them showing any sort of family of Trask's as far as Molly could ascertain.

Even above the hearth where most homes would have a family portrait, Trask had weapons. There were two swords that dominated the display, one that was as wide as Molly's hand and nearly as long as she was tall and another that was similar but smaller and which Molly had always thought of as 'feminine' crossed over it. The way the two were crossed looked to Molly as though they were embracing.

The wood floors that Molly kept polished to a glossy, high sheen glistened as Molly crossed the parlor, went through the sitting room, and entered the corridor which led to her own quarters. Somewhat removed from the master suite, Molly's chambers adjoined to it thanks to another short hallway; the arrangement having been designed by the Lady who'd owned the flat previously so that her servant could come assist her at any time of the day or night.

Here, in her private sanctuary, Molly had feminized the room considerably. Trask had allowed her to paint the wainscoting a pretty pastel pink and apply wallpaper above, which featured large dark pink cabbage roses on a lovely pale gold background. She had retained the poster-bed, desk, and wardrobe that had been in the room when she took it over, but had stripped the dark stain from them and then polished the cherry wood she found beneath to a warm reddish glow.

Molly placed her satchel on the foot of her bed and reached in to pull out a parcel wrapped in plain brown paper and tied with a thin blue ribbon tied in a small bow. Mr. Trask would never want her to think she was obligated to buy him a Christmas gift, or any type of gift for that matter, but when she'd seen that the local shop had the new Jules Verne novel, she'd saved up her extra money to purchase it for him. As he eschewed holiday decorations, there was no Christmas tree so Molly went to the entry closet and tucked it into his little-used traveling satchel so she could surprise him with it on Christmas.

The sound of water dripping into water from the bathroom drew Molly's attention and she walked over to push the slightly ajar door open. Like the rest of the flat, the bathroom was on the large side and was dominated by a massive iron claw-foot tub that must have been moved in through the window with a crane. Molly couldn't even fathom a group of men trying to wrestle the thing up the stairs!

Trask was sunk down into the tub, his arms resting along the sides on the white enameled iron and the water lapping at his chest level. His eyes were closed and Molly decided he must have fallen asleep. Shaking her head a little and breathing a sigh, Molly crossed to the tub and reached out to touch his arm to wake him.

Her fingers were still an inch or two from contact when Trask's hand suddenly had a firm hold of her wrist. Molly squeaked in fright at the unexpected movement; it had been as quick as a snake's strike and apart from his hand and arm, nothing else of him had moved. Even his eyes were still closed, Molly realized with a barely suppressed tremor of instinctive, superstitious dread.

"What is it, Molly?" Trask asked, before finally opening his eyes and tilting his head to look up at her. The way his eyes caught and held the light from the softly-hissing gas lights in the room, it was as though they were lit from within by some powerful burning energy that Molly would never understand and which scared her to the core of her being. There were times when she almost wondered if her Mr. Trask was even human.

"N-nothing, sir," Molly stammered. "I w-was just straightenin' up an' I thought you'd fell asleep."

A blink and the hand gripping her wrist let her go. "Mind your enunciation," Trask chided, his voice calm and gentle as it often was when he corrected her. "You were straightening up and thought I'd *fallen* asleep."

Molly backed away and nodded. "Yes, that's what I said," she said, relaxing marginally as the strangeness seemed to pass and Trask smiled a little.

"Hand me a towel," Trask requested as he pulled the stopper on the tub's drain and stood, his back to her.

As she complied, Molly watched him covertly. She wondered, and not for the first time, who this man really was. He was educated and refined, there was no doubting that, and clearly had money. He was also kind-hearted to have taken the time to lift her from a life that would likely lead to an early grave. However, the tattoo that covered almost the entirety of his back marked him as a man of dichotomy. The cultured façade he showed to the world was belied by the savage-looking phoenix that rose from the small of his back, its wings stretched up to just below the tops of his shoulders and its wicked beaked head residing between his shoulders.

"Thank you," Trask said as he accepted the silently-offered towel and wrapped it around his waist. "How is Lila?"

"The doctors say that her hearing will return in time, though it will never be as good as it was before," Molly replied, turning to focus on tidying up.

"What are people saying about the explosion?"

"Folks is… People in the area are saying that it was due to a rupture in the gas lines."

Trask ran his hands over the slight growth of hair on his head and sighed. "Unlikely. The house was all-but leveled. If it'd been a gas explosion, the houses adjoining it, at least, would have also been destroyed."

Molly frowned a little. "Then what do you think happened?"

Trask walked over to the vanity and rested his hands on either side of the sink, his head bowed for a moment. He then looked up, met her eyes in the mirror and said "I'm going to find out."

"Are you joking, Charlie?" Trask asked, looking up from the investigation sketches of the explosion site in the constable's notebook. The constable was on the small side and had a stocky build. His gingery hair was clipped short and his beard was just starting to show silver in it.

Charlie had the good grace to look surprised at the question, his blue eyes widening a bit. "Jerry, I'm not sure what you expect to hear here," he said, holding his hand wide. "The house didn't spontaneously explode."

"I'm not saying that it did," Trask countered with a sigh as he pushed the notebook back across to his former comrade. "There were *kids* in that house, Charlie. Don't you think they deserve an actual investigation, not just an arbitrary decision that makes no sense if you really look at the evidence. What about these other explosions? There's a link there if the brass would just let you look for it. We can't just sweep those under the rug because they weren't in upscale areas."

Charlie surged up out of his chair, his anger boiling over as he jabbed a finger in Trask's direction. "This is the sort of attitude that got you booted off the force, Jerry," he snapped. "Maybe that's fine for you, a single man with no children, but I've got a family I need to think about. I don't have a mysterious family fortune to see me through lean times because I couldn't keep my mouth shut."

As soon as the words were out, Charlie regretted them, and it showed on his face, but Trask didn't snap back. Instead, he simply nodded a little. "No, you're right, Charlie. I know that if you could, you'd push this," he said, watching his friend sink back into his chair with a defeated slump to his shoulders. "Give Siobahn and the kids my love."

Charlie summoned up a faint smile. "The kids still ask when you're going to come to dinner. I think they miss those little magic tricks you used to show them."

Trasks expression softened a bit in response to the comment and he smiled as well. "Perhaps I'll come by in a few days," he said, moving around the desk to give Charlie's shoulder a firm squeeze. "Take care of them," he said, then disappeared out the door, leaving the office seeming very empty to Charlie's eyes.

"Is she going to recover?" Trask asked as he walked with the nurse through the corridors of the sanitarium. The stench of sickness, cleansers, and despair assailed his nose and it was sheer force of will that kept him from gagging.

The nurse, a formidable blonde who looked like she'd have been right at home aboard a Viking longboat nodded. "Yes, she will, but she'll carry the scars for the rest of her life."

The woman paused outside one of the wards and looked over at Trask. "Ordinarily, I'd not let you have access to the girl, but…" she paused and the formidable expression relaxed just a little. "She's such a sweet child and she's got no family. There's no one to push for justice for her."

Trask nodded. "I'll do my best."

The woman's face hardened again. "You'd best, Mr. Trask," she said quietly, then nodded into the ward. "Bed five," she added, then turned and walked briskly away.

Trask watched the woman go with a sense of vague bemusement, simultaneously impressed with her and profoundly grateful that he never got sick. With a shake of his head, he walked into the ward.

The eyes of every child snapping to him, checking to see if it was a family member come to visit. They were eyes that were, on the whole, far too wise for their ages and he had to work to keep his face from reflecting the anger that he felt at the thought of them being cooped up in this place. He forced a smile for the kids, and then crossed to bed five.

The occupant, a small, fine-boned little girl with sandy blonde hair, was the only one who hadn't looked over in response to the opening of the door. She had no family so there would be no visitors, or so she thought. What he saw of her face revealed smooth, unblemished skin, a button-nose, and a cupid's-bow mouth.

He walked over and pulled out the chair from the desk beside her bed. The noise of the legs scraping over the tiled floor startled her and caused her to look over, revealing the scarring on the right side of her face. Her eyes were bright green with flecks of coppery brown visible in them. The beauty of her eyes, however, was mitigated by scars; the skin from her temple to her chin and from cheekbone to ear was puckered and raw, a portion of her hair seared away. The scars extended down her neck and disappeared beneath the shoulder of her hospital gown.

Trask smiled at her gently. "Hello, Miranda," he said gently as he sat. "My name is Jerry."

After a frozen moment of clear concern over whether she should speak to him, a soft "hello" was offered in return.

"I'd like to talk to you about the accident," Jerry said gently, scrupulously not mentioning the scars. He reached into the inside pocket of his suit jacket and removed a doll that he'd purchased on the way to the hospital. The doll hadn't been cheap exactly, but he hoped it would prove worthwhile. It was good quality with a stuffed canvas body, a pretty gingham dress, and golden 'hair' that could be combed and styled.

Miranda's green eyes showed new life as she saw the doll and Trask knew his instincts had been right to urge him to buy it for her. He held the doll out to her. She hesitated, her eyes going from the doll to meet his and he realized that she was fearful of reaching for it in case he pulled it away. Sighing softly, Trask reached out to tuck the doll under the blankets beside her and watched as the girl's thin arm curled around it, cuddling it close to her.

"Thank you," Miranda said, her voice a little stronger after the gift. She was quiet for a moment as she admired her new toy, then looked up at him. "Why do you want to know about the 'splosion?"

"Well," Trask said, his smile coming more easily as she relaxed a bit, "I want to find out who did this to you and see them punished for what they did. I think that whoever did this to you has hurt other kids and I want to make sure that stops."

A surprisingly shrewd expression held Trask's gaze as Miranda mulled his words over, her fingers unconsciously petting the doll's hair. Trask waited patiently, allowing her to decide for herself if she was willing to talk to him. "What if I don't want to talk about it?" she asked, her arm curling tighter around the doll, revealing her fear that he'd take it away from her if she refused.

"I'm not going to force you to speak about it if you don't want to, Miranda," Trask assured her. "If you don't want to talk about it, I'll thank you for your time and try another way."

Chewing her lip lightly, Miranda finally nodded, looking up at him again.

Trask reached out to touch her arm reassuringly and was surprised when she took his hand. Her tiny hand was eclipsed by his as he held it. "Take your time, Miranda," he advised. "I'm prepared to stay a while."

The girl nodded, and then looked over at him. "You got a family?"

Startled by the question, Trask blinked and shook his head. "No," he said, answered before he quite realized he would.

"Are you married?" Miranda asked, glancing down at his hand to see if he was wearing a wedding band.

Trask raised an eyebrow slightly at the sudden interrogation. "No." He paused, sensing that the girl was seeking some sort of commonality, and then added "I was once, but she died a long time ago."

"My mommy and daddy died a few years ago," Miranda said quietly, looking down at the weave of the blanket covering her. "Us kids in the orphanage, we decided we didn't need families... that we'd be each other's family." She trailed off and Trask let the silence stretch for almost a full minute. Just when he thought she would refuse to say anything further on the subject, she said "Timmy had a new toy he wanted to share with us."

Her voice trembling as she continued. "It was a tin man that marched around and made noise." She bit her lip hard, and then said "We were playing in the courtyard, marching the man back and forth between us. It was me and Timmy and Sean and Jenny... Sean had sent it walking over to Timmy and it started making a strange hissing and popping sound. We weren't sure what was wrong with it and Timmy was reaching out to pick it up when it 'sploded."

Quests & Answers   109

"Did he tell you where he got it?" Trask asked, watching her face.

Miranda sniffed and wiped the back of her free hand across her nose. "He said there was a man with a cart full of toys like it. Timmy said the man gave it to him, but he might've stole it."

Trask nodded and produced a handkerchief, reaching out to gently dry the tears that were rolling down her cheeks. "I'll find him," he said softly.

"Will you come visit me again?" Miranda asked, looking up at him with naked hope on her face.

Trask hesitated for a moment. "I'll try," he told her, leaning down to kiss her forehead as he gently released her hand.

Molly allowed her light grip on Trask's arm to sweep her along through the evening shopping crowds thronging the Piccadilly Circus. They'd already visited several shops, posing as a newly married couple looking for the perfect birthday gift for a nephew. Even after a couple of hours, the novelty of the simple silver band on her left ring finger hadn't worn off and she found herself unconsciously fiddling with it.

"You're fidgeting again," Trask said softly, his tone amused but not unkind.

"Sorry," Molly said, chastened. "It's just strange wearing jewelry. Where did you get this anyway? It's even the right size."

"It belonged to an old friend," Trask replied, glancing over at her. "She would've liked you, I think."

Molly smiled despite herself, and opened her mouth to ask after this friend, hoping that the generally reticent Trask would be willing to reveal more about his past, but didn't get the chance before Trask steered them into another shop.

The tiny space was absolutely packed with wares. There were carved wooden trains and animals of all descriptions, an entire wall filled with stuffed animals and plush dolls, and board games of every type. There were even, to Molly's delight, several dirigibles suspended from armatures on the ceiling which allowed them to circle and bob like the real thing.

Trask paused when he noticed Molly's reaction to the toys and chuckled softly, patting her hand before continuing further into the shop. He headed toward the soft clattering noise of gears coming from behind a display of teddy bears of all sizes, shapes, and colors and stopped in his tracks as he rounded the corner.

There were three of them, two soldiers standing about five inches tall, and a horse that stood about eight inches to the tops of its ears. They were walking about a small enclosed area on the floor, a faint bluish glow radiating from around their chest cavities where the power sources were located.

"Oh," Molly said softly, astonishment in her tone. She started to crouch down to look more closely at them, but was stopped by Trask taking her arm.

"They're charming, aren't they?" a male voice said as Trask released Molly and crouched down himself. The clerk appeared from the aisle to the right, giving Molly a smile that, Trask noticed, didn't quite reach his eyes. The man was small and thin, and rather gnomish in appearance with gaunt cheeks, large eyes and ears and almost no hair on his round head.

"Charming," Trask said, his tone carefully neutral as he straightened up and appraised the man.

"Not easy to come by either," the man said, taking Trask's comment for agreement with his statement.

Molly smiled. "We're looking for something very special for my nephew's birthday," she said.

"Oh, Miss, I daresay he'd love one of these," the shopkeeper replied with an absolutely fawning lilt to his voice. "I'm Jaime Tolliver, the proprietor, by the way."

"What do you think, honey," Molly asked, looking toward Trask who was still looking down at the toys with a difficult-to-read expression.

Tolliver appeared to notice the ring on Molly's finger and smiled. "Madam, I must apologize for not addressing you properly before. It never occurred to me that someone so young and lovely would already be spoken for, though I suppose that was foolish of me in this case. You are a very lucky man, sir," he gushed, also looking at Trask who appeared unmoved.

After a moment, Trask's eyes raised from the toys to regard the man. "How much?" he asked, meeting Tolliver's gaze.

"Oh," the little man said, pinned and discomfited by Trask's intense gaze. "Well, which one are you interested in?"

"All of them," Trask replied evenly and Molly thought the man might faint dead away.

"That would run nearly twenty pounds," Tolliver said breathlessly.

"Then wrap them up," Trask commanded, releasing Tolliver from his gaze finally and stepping back so the man could gather the toys up with shaking hands and wrap them up.

Molly looked over at Trask with a brow arched. "How *do* you do that?"

"Do what?" Trask asked, offering his arm again as his expression became pleasantly bland to escort her to the cashwrap.

"You *know* what," Molly replied, shaking her head with a bemused frown. "You have this way of looking at people that seems to scare the daylights out of them! How do you do that?"

Trask shrugged and looked over at her. "It's not something I like to do, Molly, but it's useful," he said, his tone making it clear that the subject was closed.

Molly continued to covertly watch Trask as Tolliver deactivated the toys and tucked them into a plain paperboard box, then placed the box, in turn, into a cloth shopping bag. She was grateful that she had never been on his bad side, though she did wonder, at times, what sort of man she had wound up sharing her life with, even in their relatively platonic way. She had to suppress a shiver at the idea of marrying a man with such a wealth of secrets and was grateful that their involvement was unlikely to evolve beyond friends with occasional physical liaisons.

Trask dropped Molly off at home and headed to a warehouse that he utilized as his workshop when investigating potentially dangerous items. He stood at his worktable, a heavy lead-lined apron covering his front, thick gauntlet-style gloves covering his hands and forearms, and smoke-lensed goggles protecting his eyes as he removed the largest of the inert toys, the horse, from its box.

The craftsmanship on the figure was exquisite, the joints so finely put together that they were almost entirely hidden and the animal was given almost the full range of movement of a real horse. The panel in the chest that allowed access to the power cell was also so neatly made as to almost disappear from sight, the screws securing it concealed by painting them the same roan color as the rest of the steed.

Even through the protective gloves, Trask could almost feel the energy radiating from the toy. He reached down and pulled a small vice in front of him, then secured the horse in it with its legs splayed upward, its mane and tail hanging to the table's surface down lifelessly.

He then attached an array of lenses to his goggles which would allow him to shift the magnification of his view as needed and drew the lamp closer as well before selecting a tiny jeweler's screwdriver to begin opening the casing. As the screws were extracted, deep blue light began to radiate from around the edges of the panel and Trask's frown deepened. Finally, he lifted the panel away and set it aside, the light illuminating his face more brightly than the lamp nearby.

The source of the light, and the energy to power the toy, was what appeared to be a tiny shard of crystal no larger than a grain of rice. It was held between four small clamps within the internal workings of the horse and it pulsed ever so slightly now and then. Had anyone been there to witness the scene, they would have seen an unfamiliar look on Trask's face: fear.

Trask took a moment to master his emotions, then carefully picked up a set of tweezers that were ridiculously small in his large hands, made more so by the bulk of the protective gloves. He gently prized the crystal free, unconscious of the fact that he was holding his breath until he released it in a sigh of relief when he was able to lift the shard from its housing, sliding a small bar of metal down along the tweezers so they would remain snug around the shard if he released his hold.

Holding it carefully, Trask turned from the work station and walked to the far side of the warehouse and out through the sliding door that used to serve as a livestock entrance. The remains of another warehouse that had burned down were a mere fifty feet away and that is where Trask carried his prize. He stopped at the edge of the charred corpse of the second building and threw the shard, tweezers and all into the middle. The glow of the crystal made its flight easy enough to follow in the darkness of the night, and the instant it touched the ground, it erupted into an explosion that sent debris flying away, forcing Trask to raise a forearm to protect his face and sending him staggering back several steps.

Slowly, Trask reached up to move the goggles up onto his forehead. The fear from moments ago was replaced with tightly controlled rage that hardened his face until he appeared to have been carved from granite. He remained standing at the edge of the rubble for a moment, looking down into the ten-foot-deep crater that the explosion had left behind. He thought of little Miranda and her burned face and ravaged body. He thought of a stuffed bunny lying in the roadway. He thought of the children out there potentially playing with bombs without their knowledge.

Reaching up, Trask pulled the goggles free and stalked into his workshop to lock up. He had a visit to pay and he'd have to be quick about it if he was going to catch Tolliver still at his shop.

Tolliver had just shut off the lights in the shop and was making his way to the front door when it burst open, its lock failing to remain secure when subjected to a solid kick from Trask's boot. With a squeal of fright, the startled shopkeeper turned to scurry back into the depths of the rows of shelves.

He'd gone less than five feet before a large, powerful hand dropped onto his shoulder. Trask spun him around and shoved him against the nearest shelving unit so that his back was against it, the unit rocking precariously with the impact.

"The tinker," Trask demanded, his grip painfully tight on the thin man's shoulder. "Where do I find him?"

"R-right now? I- I don't know," Tolliver protested, looking up into Trask's shadowed face like a rabbit staring into the jaws of a wolf.

Trask's eyes narrowed. "How do you contact him?"

Swallowing hard, Tolliver licked his lips. He opened and closed his mouth several times, searching for his voice, but it was only when Trask held up a sheaf of money that he found it again. "He frequents the area 'round Regent's Park, hoping to entice the mums of the upper-crust with his wares."

"No one purchases toys from this man anymore. Pass the word. Make your fellows understand. If I get word that another toy seller is stocking these items, I'll be back for you before I call on them." Trask tucked the money into the breast pocket of Tolliver's threadbare tweed jacket, then turned and strode out of the shop without another word.

Trask sat on the bench in the park, watching the young mothers and nannies, the children in their perambulators and the older ones running about playing. The occasional sound of a lion roaring or an elephant trumpeting carried from the nearby zoological garden, drawing wide-eyed looks from the children each and every time.

His eyes hidden behind smoke-darkened lenses, Trask smiled a little at the unadulterated awe that he saw in the small faces upon hearing the wild sounds. Invariably, however, the the smile faded quickly as his imagination tried to conjure up images of children who had never had a chance to be born; children who would, if the gods had been kind, had their mother's dark hair and pale green eyes.

Such musings were brought up short when a child pelted toward him, chasing after a bright red ball which bounced along the cobbled walk ahead of him. The boy looked to be no older than two and clearly mad with the heady rush of his relatively new-found mobility. His hair was almost white, it was so blonde, and contrasted sharply with the dark blue suit short-pants and jacket that he wore.

"Michael, not so quickly," a woman's voice called, that of the child's mother, no doubt.

Trask tracked the child's progress with an air of apparent disinterest. When the child's toe caught on an up-tilted cobble a couple feet away from him, however, Trask went into action. In one fluid movement, he rose from the bench, took a step forward, and crouched down to catch the child, sparing him a multitude of bumps and bruises.

"Ball!" the child protested with the sort of single-mindedness one only usually saw in toddlers and the inhabitants of sanitariums. Small, chubby hands continued to reach for the ball which bounced into the grass and came to rest against the bole of one of the massive oaks that dotted the park.

"Easy there, son," Trask said as he set the boy back on his feet while still keeping a firm hand on the tiny shoulder to keep him from bolting again. "You need to mind where you're going or you're going to hurt yourself."

"Ball!" Haughty blue eyes as bright as the summer sky glared up at Trask.

At that moment, the mother came hurrying up, breathless from chasing after the boy in the voluminous skirts which were fashionable but highly impractical for chasing after recalcitrant children. "Michael, for goodness sake! How many times do I have to ask you not to run off like that?" she demanded as she moved over to the bench that Trask had been seated on moments ago. "My apologies, sir. I have no idea what goes through his mind."

Trask gave her a gentle smile and partially rose so he could herd the child over to his mother. "No

118   *Quests & Answers*

apologies are necessary, madam," he assured her. "There was no harm done. You have a healthy and energetic boy here, which, to my mind, is a good thing. He should grow into a fine, strong man."

The woman's pale hair and blue eyes were a match for the boy's, though her features were sharper, giving her a hard, cool look even when she smiled. "Thank you, sir. You are very kind to say so," she said as she took hold of the boy to restrain him from running off again. "I just need a moment to catch my breath."

"Take your time," Trask said, turning to retrieve the ball after giving the boy over into her custody. He could feel the woman watching him, the weight of her stare an almost physical presence as she studied him.

She was well-dressed and the child was clean and well-fed, though Trask had noted the lack of a wedding band on her hand. It was likely she was a widow, then, and one that was used to being taken care of. He would have to tread carefully lest the woman try to cast him in the role of new husband and stepfather.

"Ball!" Michael crowed again, this time with rapturous joy, as Trask returned with the toy and handed it over.

"There you are," Trask said, summoning another slight smile for mother and son.

At that moment, a distinctive rattling-clicking-whirring noise caught Trask's attention. He looked down along the footpath and saw a push-cart approaching. Made of dark-stained wood with two wheels beneath, the cart had several visible doors in the sides and front for storage. There was a low railing encircling the top of the cart making it into a sort of deck where several of the risible clockwork 'toys'

Quests & Answers   119

chattered madly around. A large black oil-cloth parasol spread its black wings over the top to keep the wares protected from rain.

The man pushing the cart, the tinker that Tolliver had spoken of, Trask presumed, was surprisingly young, but had a wan, unhealthy look to him. He was tall, but stooped over at the shoulders as though borne down by a weight too heavy for him to bear. His skin was pale and had a sickly greyish cast to it as though he hadn't seen daylight in a long, long time.

His attention moved away from the young mother and her son as he watched the cart and its owner move along. Trask was dimly aware of the woman's attempts to reclaim his focus, then getting frustrated and herding the boy away with a flounce of wounded dignity.

As he watched the tinker's progress, Trask was pleased to see that most of the mothers and nannies took one look at the unwholesome appearance of the man and collected the children in their charge to herd them firmly away from him. None of those appealing little bombs would be purchased in the park today, he was confident.

But, then again, he realized that the tinker wasn't paying the mothers or the children much mind. The cart's pace was slow, but steady with no pauses near groups of children or caretakers to let them get a look at the wares. This, then, was not where he expected to sell the toys.

Trask followed the man with his eyes until he had passed Trask's position on the bench, and then got up to continue trailing along behind him at a distance. His suspicion about the tinker's clientele was confirmed as he watched the wretched looking man go from one toy shop to the next. Tolliver must have been very persuasive in passing his message along; only a couple of shopkeepers would even talk to the tinker, much less buy anything.

They walked through several different shopping areas of the city until the mid-afternoon when the tinker finally turned back toward the river, still plodding along at the placid, passive pace he'd been setting all day. Trask continued to follow, allowing himself to fall further back as the number of people around dwindled, though the tinker seemed oblivious to the idea that he might have someone trailing him.

The tinker entered a warehouse near the river quays, disappearing into the depths of it. Several moments later, he returned and stepped outside, securing the door before turning to walk away.

Trask remained in the shadows for the next few hours, watching the warehouse and waiting to see if anyone returned. As night fell, the few people out and about in the area made their way home and Trask found himself alone but for the criminals that frequented such locations for clandestine meetings.

Satisfied that his activities would go without notice, Trask left his hiding place and approached the building. The lock was new and surprisingly high quality for the area. It took him almost a minute to successfully pick it and slip into the warehouse.

The interior of the warehouse was pitch black and Trask stood by the door for over a minute, allowing his eyes to adjust. Finally, dim outlines began to resolve and he was able to make out the shape of a small oil lamp nearby. It was the work of only a second to light it and he realized that the vast majority of the windows high up in the walls had been blocked off so there was little concern about his light being seen.

The cart that the tinker had been pushing was off to the side. Most of the available floor-space in the warehouse was taken up with crates of pieces for the toys as well as raw materials and the tools needed to make the little monstrosities. Trask was horrified to see perhaps a hundred more toys lined up stacked boxes, waiting to be taken out and sold to unwitting children.

As he turned, looking at the crates, Trask stopped as a familiar blue glow leaking out of the joins of one of the crates caught his eye. Moving carefully, Trask approached it and lifted the lid, his eyes narrowing in horrified anger. Nestled into soft packing fibers were *hundreds* of the unstable crystals.

He set the lid back down gingerly and looked around for a packing list or a shipping manifest. It took ten long minutes of shuffling around the papers on the edge of the worktable to find what he was looking for. The tinker had received the crystals from an address in upstate New York, in America. The name associated with the address, however, gave Trask pause. Michael Andress.

No, Trask thought with a frown. *No, it can't be.*

And yet, in his heart, he knew. Andress, the man who'd caused the death of Trask's wife and everyone he loved. Once more, Trask's life was intersecting with Andress'. In many ways, Trask considered as he wrote down the address, it was inevitable that they would clash again. They were, after all, two sides of the same coin.

After tucking the paper into his pocket, Trask looked around the warehouse, his expression cold and calculating. After a moment of contemplation, he dropped the lamp, the oil reservoir shattering and spreading oil and flame to the dry wood of empty supply crates beside him. With that, he turned and walked quickly back out to the street.

In moments, the first explosion crashed through the quays, sending the few denizens of the area running. As Trask turned the corner a half-mile away, the fire reached the crystals and the building splintered with the force of the energy released from them.

Molly woke at her usual time. It was early yet, and she expected to have another half hour or so before Trask exited his rooms looking for coffee. Usually, she could hear him moving about by the time she finished dressing and pinning her hair, but this morning the house was eerily quiet.

With a frown on her lips, Molly made her way out to the sitting room and paused as the sensation of wrongness reached her. It took her a moment to realize that the swords that had always hung over the fireplace were missing. She knew that Trask hadn't returned home by the time she went to bed and expected to find his overcoat draped over the sofa as it usually was, but there was no sign of it.

Her unease began to turn to worry as she made her way toward the kitchen, thinking that, perhaps, she would find evidence of his having a snack upon returning to the flat in there. There, in the center of the scrubbed pine kitchen table, propped against the sugar bowl, was a large, cream-colored envelope. Her name was written across the front in Trask's angular hand.

Her heart in her throat, Molly crossed to the table and reluctantly sat down, picking up the envelope and opening it as though it might contain a poisonous snake.

The letter was short and simple:

> *Molly,*
>
> *I apologize for not saying goodbye in person, but it is imperative that I leave immediately. You have been a god-send to me these last few years and I am aware that I have not thanked you adequately for all that you do.*
>
> *My solicitor, Mr. Jenkins, will be paying you a visit in a few hours. The flat and several of my accounts are being transferred into your name. I trust that you will make good use of them.*
>
> *I fear I must ask one last service of you, dear Molly, before I bid you farewell. Mr. Jenkins will also be bringing the paperwork to facilitate your adoption of a young girl who was injured in one of the explosions that I have been investigating. She is an orphan, and a sweet child with great potential. There is more than sufficient money in the accounts to keep you and Miranda very comfortably until she has reached her majority.*
>
> *It is my wish that you care for this child, Molly. I think that you both need one another and that each of you would benefit greatly from the presence of the other in your lives.*
>
> *I shall not see you again in this life, but know that I will always think fondly of you.*
>
> *Trask*

Molly set the letter down, her worry boiling over into full-blown fear for her now-former employer. "Oh, Mr. Trask... what have you done?" she whispered to the empty kitchen.

Trask stood near the bow of the tramp freighter, looking out over the water. He was dressed in old, worn denim pants and a dingy, oatmeal colored sweater. Combined with the work boots he wore, he looked very much like a laborer who had come into enough funds to take passage to America in search of better times.

He could feel more than hear the engines working below decks, the hiss of the water sliding past the hull of the ship and the crisp snap of the American flag from where it rode near the pilot house. The smell of the coal smoke from the smokestacks was blown away from him, though he still caught a hint of it tinging the sea air. His fellow passengers were giving him a wide berth, though he barely registered them. His eyes were only for the horizon, his mind on the man who had once more intruded into his life.

His hand rested on the old, worn travel satchel that was over his shoulder. It felt heavier than he remembered, he realized, and leaned against the railing to open it. A frown darkened his expression as he saw the unfamiliar wrapped parcel, drawing it out and cautiously removing the paper.

The frown melted away into a soft, melancholy smile as he held the beautifully bound copy of *The Mysterious Island* by Jules Verne. "Thank you, Molly," he said softly, then turned to go below decks to read. It would be a long journey.

Everybody's Cousin

By Ren Cummins

Author's note: *One of the questions I've had the most about the Chronicles of Aesirium (besides whether or not there will be any more books forthcoming; and the answer to that one is "Yes"), is in regards to Cousins, and the adventure which led to his involvement with Rom and Favo and the Morrow Stone. And, while that story didn't quite fit into the narrative of the books, I was happy to submit this tale here into this anthology to shine some light on our favorite Cousin, as well as a bit of backstory to some other familiar characters. Please enjoy!*

All life in *Oldtown-Against-the-Wall* revolved around three primary structures – the colleges, the town council, and the market. The first offered knowledge, the second provided order, but the third was the most lucrative. The market spanned several blocks in every direction. It was designed like the spokes of a great wheel, with an open courtyard for an axle. Even at its extremities, families with homes at the fringes of the market had converted their living spaces into shops or the like. On any given day, even in the coldest weeks of winter, there were several dozen covered stalls open for business. Nearly anything of any imagination could be found for sale here, from the grains or vegetables and fruits grown out in the agricultural fields to livestock or meats from the stables. Given enough time, a person would encounter merchants selling tools, clothing, furnishings, and even a few stalls dedicated to the more esoteric, art-imbued items.

These last were seldom of much good – the best items were best sought by individual request from a reputable artisan – but from time to time, even the most pathetic cloud offered the possibility of rain.

Life on the streets of Oldtown was a simple enough riddle, when pondered out in the proper conditions. It could be read like a spreadsheet, numbers scratched out at the nib of a pen until a profit could at last be ascertained. Or it could be read like the schematic for a complex engine, delicately teetering on the edge between inefficiency and combustion. Taken too seriously in either direction, it became a dangerous game of cause and effect, uncertainly moving one's assets against what felt like a generally superior opponent. If it was a game, it had been designed to quench ambition and the desire to win in all but the most steadfast players. Just like its market, Oldtown provided its people with virtually whatever they might want, within reason.

The town was balanced precariously between the monolithic white wall that had been designed originally for protection and the seemingly unending and unexplored wildlands to the west. Over the years, this town of exiled practitioners of the mystic arts had fashioned for themselves a collective life of relative simplicity. Cobbling together what fundamental skills of the sciences that remained to their minds into an integrated high-pressure hydraulic matrix, they focused the rest of their minds and energies into providing for their common needs. This, they achieved though simple hard work and the passing on of those magical arts they deemed useful.

Ballis loved the market; even more than his occasional foray into the halls of the town council – at least here, there was always someone seeking his services, and unlike the other, few people here were shy about asking him. With the network of contacts and favors he had spent his life cultivating, it seemed a foregone conclusion that he'd eventually work his way to the top of Oldtown. He scoffed at this notion, however. *It'll be a barren Harvestday you see me in politics*, he thought decisively. *Give me a life without agendas and I'm a happy man. Or at least let all the agendas be my own.*

He adjusted the small cap on his head – there was just enough of a brim on it to shield his eyes from the sun which had barely risen above the Wall, marking it for just before noon. He'd already completed three tasks today, earning him a fair profit, but as far as he was concerned, the day was only now beginning.

Ballis frowned briefly as he ducked well below a cloud of steam puffing from one of the nearby copper pipes. *Nothing makes a client more nervous than seeing his contact arrive with a sweaty brow,* he thought to himself. *Even if it's just steam dotting his skin.*

He followed the rhythm of the other market pedestrians; walking too slowly or too quickly was a sure enough way to stand out. Only the one last job to wrap up today, and then he could take the rest of the day off. Granted, his interpretation of "off" merely meant that he could work the market crowds, and drum up new opportunities for business. At the tender age of fourteen, Ballis Furthore was among the more industrious people he knew. He worked at least a little each day, though some days it felt like his biggest investment involved shoe repair. He figured he walked enough to circle the town at least twice each day.

Still, each job had its rewards, he reminded himself.

Ballis reached into his satchel and drew out a small rectangular object, wrapped in a red kerchief. Letting the leather flap drop back on the bag, he casually placed the object on the center of the table in the sheltered market stall.

"Good day in the market?" he asked the purveyor.

The old man standing behind the stall looked up with a start. "Oh! Cousins, it's you! Er, yes, lad, fine day in the market indeed," he said, with a hint of uncertainty clouding his words.

Bristling inwardly at the nickname, Ballis pointed at the object on the table. "As promised," he said, giving the merchant a polite nod.

The merchant reached down with trembling hands to unwrap the cloth and examine the small box. He appeared confused for a moment, looking back up at the young man.

With an amused cock of his head, the young man smiled. "The box is free – I've got a cousin who makes them, it's just my little way of thanking you for your business. The locket your thief stole from you is inside."

"Your cousin does good work," answered the older man, pausing another moment before opening the lid. He reached in with one sun-weathered hand and pulled out a delicate silver locket, flicking the lid open with his yellowed thumbnail. Instantly, his eyes misted over with tears and a shuddering breath shook his lean frame.

"H-how-" the man stammered, overcome with emotion, "How'd you find this?"

The young man shrugged casually. "Well, it did take a bit of asking around to all the right people – and a few of the wrong ones. But I was able to stay under my budget estimates, so there's no change to my fees."

"Oh, yes, of course," the merchant said, blinking a bit of moisture from his eyes. He reached under his table for a rusty lockbox and opened it up, fished out a handful of steel coins and counted them out into the boy's outstretched and waiting hands. The coins exchanged hands before vanishing into a side pocket of the lad's waistcoat. A friendly smile and brief handshake concluded their deal.

As for the young man, he made his way once again through the market's throng, pausing to flip a coin at Braden in exchange for a ripe red fruit he plucked from his stand in passing. Behind him, the old merchant was left to appreciate the reunion with the locket he had feared was lost forever; his last physical token from his beloved wife, dead now more than ten years.

"Ah yes," Ballis said aloud to no one in particular, "this is a good day indeed. A very good day!"

On a whim, he turned to the left and nearly ran into a tall, thin man who abruptly turned to the nearest stall and tried to look thoroughly interested in the shoes being sold there. Cousins noticed a unique band on the man's right wrist – it was exposed for only a moment, but he recognized the colors that were sewn together.

The band itself marked him for membership in one of the many cooperatives that existed in Oldtown – groups of businessmen that operated in fringe functions not covered by the board of guilds. But the colors belonged to one cooperative in particular that Cousins had run across only a few times, and then only peripherally. Even that, he felt, had been closer than he liked.

Carr's Acquisitions, as they were named, was a troublesome lot. They prided themselves on existing outside of the structured affairs of Oldtown. Rumors whispered of Defense Guild payoffs trickling down into the pockets of many a member of the Constabulary, and worse. Cousins hoped they weren't suddenly taking an interest in him, but the awkwardness evident in the strange man's body language said otherwise.

Avoiding the man's gaze, Cousins moved to pass behind the man when the latter's hand snaked out and grabbed him by the wrist. Without hesitating, Cousins yelled out "Thief!" at the top of his lungs, pointing at the man with his free hand. Tall enough to be visible above the crowd of market-goers, his assailant took several moments to put together his response, which proved several moments too long. By the time he tried to assume a mask of innocence, a small circle of passers-by had already begun to form around the two of them.

Cousins raised his right foot and brought it down hard on the man's closest foot, and as he doubled over in pain, the young man raised his knee to the man's chin, sprawling him out onto the street.

"Thank you, fair citizens," Cousins said with a brief flourish. "And now, if you please, I must away!"

He was already far from the area by the time the man's pain-laced curses made their way into the general murmur of the open market.

Confident that he'd lost his pursuer, he leaned up against the brick wall behind Joden's smithy. He felt the rhythmic pounding shaking through his bones as he pulled out a tiny well-worn black leather-bound book from the satchel he wore across his shoulder. The ever-present hissing of the pressurized steam vents on the wall above him, though heavily insulated, nevertheless offered a gentle warmth that chased away the otherwise cool air. Biting through the thin membrane of the fruit's skin, he held it in his mouth while he thumbed through the pages of the book, flipping through them until he arrived at the page corresponding to that day's appointment list. He placed a final mark beside the merchant's name and scanned the rest of the unmarked names on the day's itinerary, or those yet pending resolution. *No chance of making it back into the market today*, he decided, and paused to consider his options.

The fruit nearly fell from his mouth when he felt a faint pressure on his book, and a single name slowly appeared on the next line of his schedule, as if written in an unfamiliar and invisible hand. He knew the name well enough, he'd visited her shop on more than one occasion while resolving other requests. It wasn't that he didn't like the old woman, but to his eyes she represented something around which Ballis didn't completely feel comfortable. A touch of irony, he agreed, but Ballis didn't enjoy the mystical arts, which were, after all, the basis upon which the entire town was inadvertently founded.

The schools of the arts were only available under apprenticeship, and he, a homeless youth (though much better dressed than the average), had learned all his trade upon the streets. No one was admitted to the Artisan trades without the recommendation of school or relatives. The deepest irony of all was that though many who knew him called him "Cousins", he was without any actual family to speak of.

He looked again at the name on his ledger. *Goya Parva*, he read with a sigh. Glancing to his left, he could almost make out the second floor landing of her Apothecary shop, several streets over and just to the east of Collegiate Row. Cousins shook his head, placed the book and stub of a pencil back in his pouch and took a bite of the fruit. *Might as well see what she wants,* he decided. *She evidently knows I have time to drop by.*

Keeping a wary eye out, he made his way to the apothecary as quickly as he dared.

The first thing a person noticed upon entering the shop was the aroma. Both sweet and pungent, the air nearly stung his nostrils with the variety of spices and concoctions stored in the primary storefront. Ballis knew that Goya, the old woman who was considered by many in Oldtown to be either a mystic prognosticator or moonstruck recluse, owned the entire building. She maintained the corner of the building for her store, retaining the rest for her living quarters. He hoped Goya wouldn't be here herself; her face tended to form the sort of focused expressions that made it seem like she was simply picking the words off the back of your eyes while you spoke with her.

And so it was with some relief that he saw a familiar young red-haired woman crossing the room to meet him.

"Miss...Briseida, is it?" he asked, recalling her name just in time.

She smiled, extending a hand in greeting. The skin of her hands was soft, with relatively new calluses on the pads of her thumb and fingers. *Clearly*, he surmised, *a woman from a family of relative means, only now coming to grips with the realities of labor.*

"Ballis," she said kindly. "We are glad you could come so quickly."

He let the door close behind him, and felt a momentary tingle up the back of his neck. A single brow arched on his forehead. "Wards?"

Briseida nodded. "It is for your safety as well," she said. "Madame Goya has asked me to secure your efforts on our behalf for a task of utmost discretion. It is said that you are the most reliable individual for such things."

He shrugged in response. "Well, I do know a few people, and *discretion* is one of them. How may I be of service?"

Her tension lessened, but only slightly. In spite of the glyphs cast about the room that ensured no one outside their immediate room would be able to overhear them, Briseida lowered her voice slightly. "There is an...item whose value comes from both its historical significance and its uniqueness. We need it secured and delivered to us, and kept from falling into the wrong hands."

The young man paused to assess some of the particular impressions gleaned from her request, but was interrupted by the realization that they were not alone in the room. Glancing past her, he noticed a gentleman seated in a simple wooden chair on the far side of the room. Thin and apparently tall, the man sat cross-legged, seemingly engaged in the contents of an old book propped up on his lap. While turning the pages with his left hand, his right rose to casually scratch the thin brown beard that accented the angle of his jawline. Ballis cocked his head, deliberately drawing attention to the presence of this other person, addressing the fact that Briseida had neglected to introduce him.

She turned around in the direction of his gaze, nodding briefly. "This is another associate of mine; he can be trusted to maintain our confidence."

Ballis shrugged. "Far be it for me to question it," he said wryly. "Regardless, I have a few concerns with this request already, and you haven't even provided the particulars. This by itself is an additional concern."

"Speak your mind, lad," the seated man said. His voice was soft and low but carried well across the room.

With a contented nod, the young man responded. "First of all, you must know by my reputation that I prefer to arrange work, and keep myself functionally distant from any hands-on activities. Second, the Arts are involved here, and I am generally uncomfortable around such dealings, though, as you likely know, I do on occasion make exceptions. Thirdly, I don't generally cater to thievery. On the other hand, Algus Breadmore is a fool, and anything that would choke that foul man's blathering maw would bring a smile to my face."

Briseida's mouth hung open. Behind her, the seated man laughed warmly. "Your reputation is well-earned, lad," he said. "Bree, I think you have your answer."

She stammered, "How – what did…" Her face took on a more serious mien. "Tell me how you know this."

To his merit, Ballis managed to conceal his smugness from his face and voice. "I am aware of the connections Madame Goya possesses in the colleges; any artifact possessed by them or any of the guilds would not require such acts of subterfuge as this. In fact, were your wish to secure an item through legal means, there are far more well-established agents in the markets or upon the town council. I am disconnected from the merchant's network and essentially independent, so the only reason you might seek to secure my services would be because you wish to acquire an item through…alternate means."

He paused again for effect – and to continue ascertaining the accuracy of his statements off their faces. "On the other hand, there are many far more skilled cracksmen available than I, and in financial ranges both higher and lower. So, removing financial and experiential criteria, that leaves a skillset or attribute specific to me. I am well-known to have no truck with the Arts, so clearly this rules out targets whose homes or offices favor such things and yet might seek to possess such items in the first place. This leaves only a handful of individuals. I myself am strongly allied with *two* of these, thus prohibiting my involvement. Of the two remaining, Belarius Gertick has a security force that rivals the Defense Guild, and you would know I would never accept a job to pick that pocket. That leaves the Breadmore manor, and it wouldn't take a seer to know there's no love lost between he and I."

Seeing no objection from the others, he went on, adding, "This merely leaves three points of business: how soon you require the item, the nature of the item itself, and what you're willing to pay for my services."

The older gentleman set his book down and leaned forward from the deeper shadows, a mischievous smile on his lips. "You wouldn't perform this task for the sheer satisfaction of repaying an old debt?"

Ballis scoffed. "There is business and there is pleasure, sir. Only a fool confuses the two."

"And you are no fool?"

The boy shrugged. "I don't confuse the two."

Briseida nodded her head approvingly. "The opportunity for acquiring this object is brief – we believe others may be en route to take it for themselves. And in addition to the standard fees we understand you request for this sort of thing, Goya has offered a few items from her collection which you may find both valuable and useful." She lifted a small bag from a shelf beside her and held it out for Ballis.

Tentatively – so as to not appear too interested – he reached up and took the bag, taking a moment to feel its heft. It was relatively light, but solid, whatever was in there. He unwound the binding and looked inside; his brows wrinkled as he reached in and pulled out two items. The first item appeared to be a short, leather-bound stick not much longer than his hand. One end was capped with a flat cross-piece of iron, making the item look like a sword that was missing its blade. The other item was a triangular-shaped box that opened up to reveal four polished marbles, one at each point, and one in the center. He passed his hand over the different-colored stones; the three around the central red stone were white, brown and blue. Ballis shook his head, smiling. "The Elemental Path, I see. Arts of some sort?"

Ian nodded. "Air, water, soil and fire, yes. They each have a few uses, so I wouldn't suggest throwing them too far away."

Ballis picked up the blue stone, which was quite cool against his fingertips. "How....how do these work? And what exactly do they do?"

After guiding his hand back down to carefully release the stone back into its position, Briseida explained, "They will do what you need them to, within reason, based upon the elements that have been focused into them. You only need hold them and will them to action."

He removed his hand from the top of the case as if it had threatened to bite him. After a moment's hesitation, he took the box and placed it carefully into his shoulder bag. The other item, he took in his right hand, balancing and weighing it. His eyes delivered an unspoken question towards Briseida and Ian.

"It is a device of my own design," Ian explained. "I haven't named it yet, but I think of it as a kind of skeleton key, but for fighting."

"But there's no blade," Ballis said, superfluously.

"You're not fighting."

"So there'll be a blade...when I need it?"

"Yes."

"But not until then?"

"Yes."

Arching an eyebrow, Ballis shook his head. "But it will *definitely* be there when I need it, you say."

"Indeed."

The young man took a long breath, releasing it in a sigh. "Well, here's to hoping I can use it in good health."

"That's the spirit."

With a faint shaking of his head, Ballis muttered something about "inspiring confidence," and placed the *Hilt of Most Likely Definite Good Health* into his bag and affixed what he hoped was a pleasant smile on his face as he looked back up to Briseida.

"So, where is this object that has so enthusiastically drawn your attention?" he said, now content to just take the particulars and get this job over with.

* * * * *

Algus Breadmore was a second-generation businessman, now in the latter half of his sixth decade. A man who'd scarcely built upon the legally-appropriate successes of his father, Algus did what any relatively unscrupulous man with the available assets and genetically superior physical frame might do: turn to a life of organized crime. Without the unpleasant constraints of morality or a disposition towards a patient growth of personal economy, Algus rose quickly past many of the less ambitious organizations at his perimeter to stake his claim on several cornerstones of the black market in Oldtown. And although he was well known for his unusual disdain for the Arts, he financed one of the largest private militias in the town, if not *the* largest.

While a sizeable number of them were spread about the town in order to maintain his communications and service network, his estate, a four-story grand edifice on the southern border of the population center of Oldtown, was constantly patrolled both within and without by an impressive display of well-trained and well-armed soldiers.

Ballis sighed. *This is not going to be easy*, he told himself for the third time in as many minutes. To Algus' mind, fear and greed required him to create a physical force to repel any potential threats. Fear, like a disease, was contagious, and this same fear infected the men themselves. They were filled with aggressively nervous energy and clearly considered anyone on the streets a possible combatant.

This contrasted powerfully with the fact that Algus Breadmore seemed to want, above all else, social acceptance. This was evidenced by the grand parties he threw in his estate nearly every week. That pretention was the one chink in his otherwise flawless armor, and Ballis was happy enough to exploit it.

With a faint smile, Ballis adjusted the collar of his button-up shirt and ran the palms of his hands down the front of his waistcoat to smooth it. Confidently, he strode directly up to the slowly-evolving line of attendees, watching and listening to all the conversations around him.

The guards were stationed about the estate, carefully chosen based on their appearance and disposition. The rougher, less personable (or less intelligent) ones were positioned in the rear of the estate, overseeing the comings and goings of the staff and delivery services. As he had no room in his budget to fabricate the sort of high-end food or drink that Algus would have delivered to his parties, Ballis knew that wasn't his entrance.

More aggressive and physically fit soldiers were placed around the defensive perimeter of the complex, and no manner of eloquence could get him past them.

But the front door was another matter altogether. As the attending dignitaries began to arrive, the soldiers at the front door were assigned based upon their people skills, with an emphasis on good looks rather than combat prowess. However, the best element of their professional demeanor was an overriding dedication towards making it appear to the guests as if nothing was ever wrong.

As he moved to the front of the line, one of the guards eyed him suspiciously. "Ain't no kids invited to this party," he said just loudly enough for Ballis to hear him. "Best scarper, boy."

With a deferential laugh, Ballis shook his head. "Not here for the festivities," he said. "I was sent by my aunt to deliver a message here for her son. Is Carso working back in the kitchen tonight?" Carso was a year older than he was; Ballis had gotten into a fight with him a few months back, and he'd been waiting for an opportunity to drop his name into a situation that might offer a bit of payback.

The guards half-greeted another pair of guests as they passed, obviously hoping to be rid of this young man as quickly as possible. "Carso? Don't know him."

Ballis was about to respond, but the other guard cut him off. "No, I know the boy. About your size, yes?"

"A bit taller. Darker hair," Ballis shrugged. "Gets that from his dad."

The second guard nodded. "Right, well, he's working, sure enough. But that doesn't get you in."

With a pat of his shoulder bag, Ballis nodded. "His ma sent me over to see that he gets his ointment," he said, lowering his voice confidentially. "He's not meant to touch food without it, on account of the *rash*."

That stopped the guards cold, and it took the first guard a few moments to answer. "Fine," he growled, extending a hand. "Give it over, I'll see he gets it."

Ballis nodded, opening his satchel. He pulled out a clay bottle, sealed with a cork; before placing it in the guard's outstretched palm, he also fished out a pair of gloves and a folded cloth. "You'll also need these to apply it; it's not really someplace easy, if you get my meaning. And don't mind the pus, it goes away with a bit of fresh water--"

The guard looked fit to throw up right there; he stepped back quickly, gesturing for Ballis to put the items back. "Well, we're pretty busy here anyway, why don't you go on back and do it yourself?"

With a casual shrug, the lad did so. "That's probably for the best," he said, dropping the items back in and replacing the cover flap. "Carso gets ever so shy about this." The guards stepped quickly aside to let him pass.

Waving briefly, Ballis turned and walked up the short stairway and through the opened doors. To his right was the servants' passage, to the left were the stairs, leading up to the bedrooms, study and library. The clock on the far wall above the double doors leading into the ballroom indicated only a few minutes before the hour. *All I'll need, Reapers willing. Assuming they're bothering to watch, that is.* He paused just long enough inside the doorway to force a few people to pause behind him and block him from view of the guards, then turned left and made his way leisurely up the stairs.

The trick to getting around in places you aren't welcomed, he had long since learned, *was to act like you belonged there. Nothing betrays you more than your own insecurity.*

At the landing, he moved along the inside wall, letting the banister block him from view. In addition to the wooden supports, Algus had instructed his servants to suspend long and gaudy tapestries from the rail, offering a pleasant wall of concealment for Ballis. He counted the doors as he passed them, finally arriving at number six.

The main foyer beneath him wasn't large; only a dozen or more people milled about on their way to the other side of the room where they faded into the general noise of music and sounds of conversations. All the same, opening this door was sure to get him some unwanted attention, whether by sound or motion. He crouched down beneath the doorknob and reached up to test it. The knob turned roughly a quarter of the way before coming to an obstructed halt. Ballis sighed, shaking his head. *Thank the Shepherds I had 'cousin' Bardac teach me the finer points of locksmithing.*

Inside the pouch, he found the devices Bardac had given him for this sort of thing – a thin hollowed-out object which looked like a toothless key, and an iron rod with what appeared to be a tube and a pair of wings at one end. Ballis placed the key into the lock, slowly, until it came to rest at the interior wall of the mechanism. He then slid the second piece into the inside of the key, until it stopped as well. Then, with a calming breath, he pressed the two wings between his thumb and forefinger. A soft hiss from the tube filled the keyholes with a faint burst of rapidly-released steam which forced the individual tumblers to click into place. Before the pressure relented, he gave the key a steady turn. The lock shuddered once and then slid back into the housing.

Suddenly, the clock in the main foyer below him rang out, pealing a series of chimes that were displayed in the very center of the ceiling. Ballis counted four beats, and then turned the knob as the highest chime resounded through the hall, masking the sound. In one motion, he pulled the key out and pulled the door shut again by the next beat of the chimes, only turning back and breathing a brief sigh of contentment before setting himself to his next challenge. *They said the item is secreted inside an old book; shouldn't be too hard to suss out,* he thought confidently.

The room was dark; he reached into his bag and pulled out the triangular box. Holding it flat on the palm of his hand, he opened it and pulled out one of the central stones – *I don't need anything actually on fire; here's hoping I can just coax some light out of this.*

No sooner had he thought it then the marble began to shine with an extreme incandescence – so brilliant that Ballis had to roll it into the palm of his hand while he fumbled with the wooden lid that contained the other stones. *This is why I hate the arts*, he thought. *Too unpredictable.*

With the box back in his satchel, he carefully revealed the stone, letting a bright beam of light pour from the circular space created by the space between his coiled thumb and forefinger. "Oh, damn," he whispered. Around him, illuminated by the cone of warm light, was what had to be an entire library of books of all shapes and sizes, on columns of bookshelves that reached from floor to vaulted ceiling and covered nearly every square meter on each of the room's four large walls. He sighed again. *Might as well start looking*, he whispered to himself, and began by looking for any books left out, or displayed prominently about the room.

A desk near the far side of the room was covered a small stack of books, stacked in no apparent concern for their protection. That seemed as good a place to start as any, and Ballis didn't relish the thought of climbing the bookshelves and pulling each book out in turn to see if they held what he was looking for.

The title of one of the top books leapt out at him, though, "Mysteries of the Machines." His mind turned to the old husks of constructs that had once served the people of Oldtown, but now only existed by the presence of a few long-abandoned and partly-rusted objects strewn about out beyond the agricultural fields. Glancing across the others, they all seemed to be pertaining to the same sort of historical nonsense – books going at length in the descriptions of that lost knowledge. He shook his head. *Old Science and strange artifacts, what are you doing, Algus? Other than losing your precious sensibilities, that is.*

Of all the books, however, one stood out from the rest. Where all the others dealt with the old Machine lore, one of the books on the desk, besides being substantially of a more recent printing, was entitled "Barter and Taxation Codes". His free hand was reaching for it before it even occurred to him. Once he lifted it, he knew he'd found it, the heft was all wrong for a book of this size. He put it back down and flipped it open, turning the pages in chunks until he found section wherein an oval section had been cut free, offering a snug hiding place for a golden and semi-opaque egg-shaped stone. It was large enough to fit in the palm of his hand, not small enough to completely enclose his fingers around it.

As he picked it up to place into his back, the stone in his other palm flared, becoming at once incredibly hot. With a surprised "ouch!" he dropped the fire marble, and the room returned to darkness. The other stone in his left hand continued to glow, however, but much less brightly than the fire marble. He held the egg-shaped stone over the table until he found the marble, and delicately touched it. It was as cool as it had been when he'd first held it, if not colder still. Picking it back up, he thought of the light again, but nothing happened. He shook his head. *Some trick*, he thought. *Thing was supposed to have a few spells cast into it, but I think I broke it. That, or it was a poor thing to begin with.* His eyes returned to the larger stone, still in his left hand, and a shiver crossed his spine. *Or maybe this had something to do with it,* he reasoned. He nodded, convinced. *At any rate, that concludes this portion of my grand adventure, now I simply need to make my way out.*

The smirk that had crept onto his face vanished instantly at hearing a sound outside the door. It was a combination of low, hushed voices and a tentative grip on the doorknob. Standing as he was behind the desk, there were no other more readily available places to secret himself, nor time to look for them. He dropped to the floor and rolled beneath the relative concealment of the desk, thrusting his hand with the egg-shaped stone into his satchel in an effort to once again engulf the room in darkness.

A moment later, the door opened, a broad band of light cutting a swath across the room and shining on the room behind his hiding place. Two figures stood in the doorway; a man and a woman.

The woman was speaking; her voice was casual and conversational. "I mean it, Favo, go back down and enjoy the party, no sense in both of us wasting our evening looking for some rubbish stone." Ballis nearly gasped. Though he'd never met the man, Favo's name was well-known on the streets. He'd even seen him once, from a distance, and Ballis had made a point to give the man a wide berth. Whispers on the street suggested that he'd climbed to near the top of Oldtown's underground crime network on the backs of a score of the bodies of his former competitors.

"Shhh," came the man's voice. On the back wall, Ballis could make out the silhouettes of both people. The man extended an arm to the right. "Light's over there, be careful."

"Careful? Think I can't make my way across a dark room?"

"No, love, I'm confident your many skills include the cautious navigation of a bit of rogue furniture

Quests & Answers

across an unfamiliar landscape," Favo said after a long pause. "But I suspect that we might not be entirely alone here."

"You're sure?" the woman asked.

"Algus never leaves this door unlocked," he said. "Any thief worth his shoes would have locked the door after him. At least," he amended, "*I* would have."

Ballis carefully tucked the presumably yet-glowing egg-shaped stone into the bottom of his satchel and into one of the soft leather gloves he kept there, and drew out another of the elemental marbles. In the darkness, he couldn't tell which of the three remaining objects he had grabbed, so he simply grabbed all three. Until he needed the item to be activated, he kept his mind clear, concerned that any particular thought might trigger it preemptively.

He could hear soft, hushed footsteps approaching on the carpet. His heart pounded in his chest.

Eventually, the steps paused beside the desk he was hiding beneath. Something small and metallic knocked against the wood.

"Come out, boy," the woman said. "We saw you sneak into the party, we know it's you."

A strangely elegant black boot pushed the chair aside, and the wearer leaned closer. Dark hair evidently lightened by time under the sun was lightly mussed in a manner Ballis assumed to be in fashion, and crisp blue eyes peered in at him. "Why, hello there, lad. I believe I recognize you now. They call you 'Cousins,' correct?"

Favo extended a hand down towards the young man. With the marbles still concealed in his left fist,

Cousins ignored the offered hand, and crawled out to stand between the two of them. He glanced briefly at the woman, tried to size her up quickly as a potential threat. She was just shorter than Favo, with tall boots and a white, fur-lined jacket that buttoned at the waist and extended down to the backs of her knees. Her bold red hair was kept back from her face by a pair of dusty riding goggles that rested upon the crown of her head. Visible beneath the jacket was a low-slung double holster; one of the weapons was drawn and leveled at his face. He'd heard of the *spellshot,* a weapon which held and discharged cartridges of art-infused energy, but had never seen one this close.

"Molla," Favo whispered, "please. The boy isn't our enemy, we needn't treat him as such. You're merely making him nervous, and I would never want a friend – we are friends, aren't we, Cousins? – to be put in a position to make decisions under duress."

Clearly reluctant, Molla nevertheless conceded, holstering the weapon.

"Good girl," the man said, somehow managing to sound both sincere and condescending in the same breath. Turning his full attention back to Ballis, he held out his hand, palm up. "Now, then, since I assume you already have the item we all have come seeking, why don't you do yourself the greatest favor I could possibly imagine and give it to me."

To his own surprise, Cousins did nothing. After the first moment of non-response, he realized that each additional moment would simply increase the tension of the room exponentially, but still couldn't bring himself to turn the stone over to them. *Why not?* He thought. *It would mean failing to do my job, which, while a rare thing, wouldn't be the first time, either. Is it pride? Am I that stubborn that I would risk my own life just to not be beaten by this ruffian?*

Favo slowly began to shake his head. "You're not that stupid," he said. "You don't really have a choice; we're leaving with the stone, and whether you're alive or dead when we do that is the only option you have. Though," he said, a thoughtful expression emerging on his face, "I wouldn't be disinclined from sweetening the pot. To be honest, I could use someone with your skills in my organization. You're clever, well-connected and have a good reputation on the street – something I lack, to my deep and abiding regret." He turned his hand onto its side as a gesture of partnership.

Again, Ballis wondered why he simply couldn't reach in and pluck out the stone, and hand it over to them. But something troubled him about the notion of giving this over to Favo. It was something in Briseida's eyes, he realized, that odd sense of concerned urgency that she had been feeling with respect to this stone. It was a dread realization that, whatever this item was, it was an essential and likely dangerous thing to fall into the wrong hands. His eyes looked back to Favo's hand; it was steady, not shaking. When he looked back up to Favo's face, their eyes met and Ballis realized that his own chances of getting out of this situation alive were declining rapidly. He'd need to do something, and quickly.

Favo's eyes darted downwards and took note of Ballis' left fist. A smile broadened on his face. "Last chance, boy," he said. Molla took a step to her right, placing him between her and the desk. Favo mirrored her movement, standing beside her with his hand still outstretched. Cousins' hand rose, seemingly of its own volition, the back of his fist facing the floor. His eyes darted with a deliberate languor past the barrel of Molla's weapon. He knew a little about the spellshots, enough to know that they required a verbal command; the wielder had to say a word that directed the energy from the released Art in order for it to work. An idea formed.

A thick, cold swelling began to fill his fist, darkening the spaces between his fingers. He held it as long as he dared. When he looked back up at the two older criminals, their eyes also moved from his fist to his face. A spot of confusion appeared on Favo's brow, giving Cousins one final thrill of victory before he unleashed the explosion of dirt and water. Emerging as an enormous and focused mud ball, Cousins channeled the water and soil marbles into a single burst of viscous brown matter, emphasizing its destination: Molla's face. The moment before it struck, her spellshot was already back in her hand and drawing a line towards Ballis' face. The glowing shell flew out of the barrel and bounced harmlessly off Cousins' chest, the required command being choked off by a mouthful of mud.

He half-turned back towards the desk and placed his right hand atop it, kicking off from Favo's stomach and vaulting towards the door.

Behind him, he could hear the sounds of Molla's coughing while Favo's voice barked out a single command: "Shut!" The door ahead of him began to swing back towards the frame, but Cousins held up his left hand and pushed out a single burst of air in that direction, the force of which blew the door from its iron hinges.

As he rounded the corner, Molla managed to pull off a few more attempts. Her voice was nearly screaming the three shots: "Stop! Stop! *DIE*!"

The second shot struck his right foot, knocking him off-balance and sending him over the banister as the third shot disintegrated the chandelier in the main foyer. The floor came speeding up to catch him, but Cousins managed another blast of the air marble directly beneath him, slowing his fall at the last possible moment. He landed hard, but without injury. His right foot, numb from Molla's weapon, forced him to a hurried limp as he made his way as quickly as possible from the room, as panicked partygoers ran in all directions. As he passed through the doorway, he sent a final burst of soil into the air, which filled the room with an obscuring dust that masked his getaway.

By the time Favo and Molla found themselves at the exit, Cousins was nowhere to be found. Favo couldn't hide an appraising smile as he patted the inconsolably livid Molla. "Fret not, my love, this is only a temporary thing. Poor lad still has to deliver it, thus we merely need to lie in wait."

With a second glance at Molla, he stifled a chuckle, adding, "But first, you'll want to clean up."

He turned, walking over to a two-wheeled compressed steam-drive vehicle which he'd left parked nearby, and, in so doing, missed the expression of pure rage that momentarily darkened Molla's face.

* * * * *

Cousins peered out the wooden slats of the tiny window and looked over the street. It was moving on towards noon, and the streets were more crowded. He'd slept in the cramped loft overnight, realizing he was too defenseless on his own with Favo and Molla hot on his heels. He'd managed to lose them at Algus's estate, but their arrival at the very moment he was preparing to take the item was too convenient to be coincidence. Any movement he made on the streets was bound to be tracked. The chances of either being intercepted or being followed to the Apothecary were too high to risk it. Better, he thought, to let enough time pass that they suspect him of already delivering the stone, re-think their assumptions, and give him a window of opportunity to slip past their notice and actually make the delivery.

He also decided that it wouldn't hurt to wait until there were more people around to mask his movements. While he waited, he pulled out the large stone again to get a better look at it. It was no longer glowing as brightly as it had last night, but still felt slightly warm to the touch. *Strange rock*, he thought. *Who would've thought something so small could stir up so much excitement?*

He pulled an extra box from his bag and looked at the two items side by side, gauging them for size. Content, he opened the box and placed the stone inside of it. It was what his 'cousin' called a secret box. There was a trick to opening it, which required pressing on two separate panels at the same time to trigger the latch. He put a piece of cloth into the box first, and wrapped the stone in the cloth to prevent it from moving around inside the box before closing it securely. He shook his head. *This masks the symptoms, it doesn't cure the disease. Maybe I shouldn't have taken this job.*

The crowds were finally beginning to thicken, and Cousins decided that if there were ever a good time to try and make his way to the apothecary, this was probably it.

He dropped down from the loft crawlspace into the pantry below, and, after re-concealing the hatch, dusted himself off and stepped out into the street, closing the door behind him. The small room above Carstin's Mercantile was one of the few secured safe-rooms he kept aside for times of the most challenging and dangerous need. *There was no chance that –* he stopped dead in his tracks. At the intersection of streets ahead of him, he could see Favo coming in his direction.

Favo and Molla were on Favo's two-wheeled vehicle, driving slowly while Favo glanced frequently at some small device in his hand. *He's tracking me, somehow*, Cousins realized with a grimace. *Time to run.*

Turning around, he ran straight into a pair of girls, knocking one over and tangling himself up in the process. He looked up at them – the one he'd knocked down was perhaps the most shockingly beautiful girl he'd ever seen, though her patchwork clothing marked her for an orphan, like her friend. But her friend, who was even then helping her to her feet: he knew her.

"Oh. Cousins," she said.

He felt a knot in his stomach tighten. It wasn't safe here, he realized. He got up and ran back towards his hiding place without another word. Not even daring to peek out, he focused on trying to slow his breathing and calm himself down.

A few moments later, he heard hushed voices, and nearly bolted until he realized it was the two girls, hiding in front of the very doors he was himself hiding behind. If they stayed out there, he knew it was only a matter of time before Favo saw them and intimated that he might be here. On the other hand…something told him that this might be more than simple providence. *Perhaps a case of Reaper's Luck, for good or ill. Right now, I'll take any luck I can get,* he decided, and opened the door to speak to the two girls.

Several minutes later, he'd sent the girls on their way, having found a happy agreement that suited them all, and it was a much less fearful Ballis that made his way through the marketplace. In the back of his thoughts fluttered a young girl's face, her dark eyes posing a perplexing distraction.

When he felt a strong hand take him by the shoulder, he managed to betray an appropriately manufactured expression of concern and surprise. Molla looked to be the angrier of the two, but Cousins wasn't sure if that was better or worse.

"Got you!" she spat.

Cousins made a substantial display of discomfort, looking around them. "A bit public, isn't it, for an execution?"

Favo laughed convivially. "My boy, you are too big a fan of the dramatics. Why, we're only just in time for a lunch and a proper conversation between businessmen." He nodded to Molla, who, in spite of her obvious frustration, led the way through the crowd, Favo keeping a firm hand on Cousins' arm.

Stealing a glance at Favo's face, Ballis had to admit he was fairly impressed by the degree of projected calm the older man wore. No one seeing the trio walking through the market would have reason to suspect them of trouble; he nodded and saluted the shopkeepers on their way, calling most of them by name and briefly asking after their family members while they passed. If any of them happened to notice the boy being almost dragged along with them, no one seemed to think twice of it.

After a few minutes of walking, they left the general hubbub of the market behind them, and Cousins began to wonder (and not for the first time, nor the last) if all this risk was worth the price of that stone. But, he reminded himself (not for the first nor last time) that it was not truly the stone he was protecting, but his reputation. Failure was a sure way to lose any hope of return business.

Then again, so is dying, he thought.

Favo pointed Molla towards Favo's vehicle, propped up against a nearby building. "Take it on ahead and meet us at the storage, Cousins here and I need a bit of man-to-man time. There's a dear," he said casually.

With a curt nod of her head, Molla did as she was bidden. Once she had vanished around a corner two streets up, Favo released Cousins' arm. "Don't run off," he advised. "I'm not above shooting you in the back."

"Wouldn't think of it," Cousins lied. "Lead on."

Favo gestured down the street in the direction Molla had departed, and they resumed walking.

"I won't waste your time, I only ask you not waste mine," Favo began. "I know you took the stone, and you know I won't stop until I have it. Are we both agreed on those two points?"

Cousins nodded. "Yes, on both counts, but you're wrong for thinking I still have it."

Favo sighed. "Perhaps, but you haven't delivered it yet, have you?"

"What makes you think I haven't?"

The older man laughed. "For starters, you're still rummaging about in this rubbish heap. With the amount of coin that trinket's worth, you could buy your way back into the City."

Scoffing, Cousins shook his head. "Who says I'd want to go? For that matter, who says they're even selling the opportunity?"

Favo looked down at Cousins, his blue eyes seemingly trying to read the boy's mind. He sighed. "I'm not certain I approve of your lack of ambitions, boy."

"I sleep well enough at night."

"And, see, Cousins, there's the problem," Favo said wryly. "Nighttime is precisely where the best work happens; you sleep through it, you miss it all." He waved his hand to cut off Cousins' anticipated response. "But that's irrelevant. My point is, we're at an impasse here; one which I am at a loss for how to resolve. We both have made promises to our employers to deliver a single item, and clearly only one of us will be able to make good on our word."

"True," Ballis agreed.

"And I'm similarly assured that you are not the type to forgo your work, therefore I have a counterproposal: namely, that we both make good on our agreements."

"I suspect there's going to be part of this I won't like, but go on and share your plan."

Favo nodded. "Perhaps. I simply ask that you go on and deliver the charge to your employer, but let me know who it is that has paid you off. And then Molla and I will take it from their hands after the fact. That way, we both receive our rewards."

Cousins was already shaking his head before Favo finished his pitch. "Even assuming for a moment that I would betray my employers, which you should know I would not do, there is no good way to arrange such a bit of information. If I tell you in advance, you would simply stake out the employer and steal the item before I could make the exchange. The only other logical option would be for you to trust that I would tell you their identity after the exchange has been made."

"Which I would not do," Favo concurred. "As I said, an impasse. How do you suspect we will surpass this, then?"

They reached the corner and turned right. "I see no solution that profits us both, nor one that prevents harm to either of us."

With a sigh, Favo nodded his head in agreement. "Regrettably, I must confess I see no other way, either." He turned to face Cousins, wearing an expression of genuine regret. "It has been an honor working against you, young man." In his hand, a spellshot pistol was raised at about waist-height.

"I doubt honor had aught to do with it," Cousins replied.

Favo shrugged, pulling the trigger. The spellshot fired, a glowing cartridge of compressed Art being cast from the barrel and bouncing harmlessly off Cousins' waistcoat.

Cousins blinked, clutching his chest and realizing nothing had happened. He looked back up at Favo, whose expression was now blank. A piece of rigid paper was stuck to his shirt which hadn't been there a moment before.

"Reaper's *breath*!" he exclaimed. "Thought you had me dead to rights, old chap."

"Closer than I would've liked," came a familiar voice over Cousins' shoulder. "I missed the hand, but I stopped the tongue."

Cousins turned to see Ian striding casually towards him, placing a small rectangular box back into the interior of his jacket.

"We should go," Ian said, tapping the piece of paper, which dissolved into dust at his touch. "He'll be back to his wits inside of a minute; we shouldn't be here when that happens."

With a final glance back at the inexplicably statue-like criminal, Cousins broke into a run to keep up with Ian.

When they at last finished running, Cousins leaned over to brace himself up with his hands on his knees as he struggled for breath. He raised his head, briefly wiping the sweat off his brow with the back of his hand. Ian looked around, seeming content that they had avoided being followed. Cousins noticed that the older man seemed no worse for wear; he didn't look as if he'd been running at all.

He glanced down at Cousins, nodded at something of which only he was aware, and reached into the patchwork jacket he wore and drew out a tall wooden cup, handing it to Cousins. "Here, you should drink some water before you pass out," he said.

His throat was burning enough that he didn't initially question where the cold cup had come from. The water was almost shockingly icy on Cousins' throat, and he felt almost instantly better. He handed the cup back into Ian's outstretched hand, and tried to keep his eye on it as Ian passed it behind his right arm for but a moment. However, when his left hand returned to view, the cup was gone.

Before Cousins could say a word, a nearby pressure junction sprayed up a prolonged blast of steam into the sky, loudly enough to cut him off.

Ian smoothed out the fabric on his jacket. "Well, young man. I can only assume that as those two had some shenanigans lying in wait for you, you were successful in your task?"

Cousins nodded, his mind still wondering about the wooden cup.

"Excellent news, lad! Very well, then, I should probably take that...oh." Ian's expression drooped. "You don't have it anymore."

"No, sir," Cousins replied. "I needed to get it someplace safe so that they couldn't find it on me."

Ian laughed. "And you gave it to the one person I should have liked to have kept it far from," he said. He waved his hand, cutting off Cousins' response. "No, that's a question for another day. First, we shall need to make arrangements. We'll need to get them to meet us somewhere that your ruffian friends won't try and follow. Someplace…" Ian looked towards the west. The agricultural fields were visible between the streets, and, beyond them, the lush and dangerous greenery of the Wild. "I know an area that might work," he said at last. "Can you deliver a message to Romany?"

Furrows appeared across Cousins forehead. "How do you know Rom?" he asked.

"Long story, too long for today, maybe later," he smiled. "And her friend, too, the smith."

Cousins could feel a bit of a flush appearing in his cheeks. "The smith? You mean Kari?"

Ian's smile deepened. "Oh yes, that one. She's a part to play as well, we'll have to invite her along."

"I can get them a message, yes. But wouldn't it be simpler to just go to them and get the stone?"

"No," Ian said with a faint shake of his head. "It's not time, yet. Two days should be about right, perhaps three."

"If you insist," Cousins said. A strong scent of sugar and chocolate passed his way, drawing his attention to his right. Auran's Confectionaries, he read on the sign. An idea formed. "Ah, I have an idea for getting a message to them," he said.

"Perfect! We have a few hours before it gets dark, come. We need to locate the perfect place to perform the exchange."

He began leading the confused Cousins towards the fields. "Wait," the young man said as they walked. "You're not thinking about having us all meet up out in the Wild?"

"I am."

"But that's too dangerous! We need to figure out a different place - one of them could be hurt, or worse."

Ian's expression grew dark, and, Cousins thought, a little sad. "I know," he replied, stopping to address Cousins directly and somberly. "But that's how it always begins."

They lay low for a pair of days, with Cousins grumbling about "lost business and diminished reputation" and Ian ensuring that the lad stayed safely in Goya's house. Cousins spent the time reading from Goya's extensive library. To everyone's delight, the two days eventually came to an end, and the two men left Goya's apothecary under cover of night.

"Looks like rain," Cousins said with a frown. "I should have brought a jacket. And larger boots, perhaps."

The two were trudging through the packed dirt of an access path between two of the square hectometers of tilled soil, the darkened silhouette of the thriving Wilds growing steadily before them. To his imagination, the mountains far off to the west had already swallowed up the sun, and now the overgrowth was doing the same in turn to the mountains. In a few minutes, it would swallow them up as well. The thought made him shiver nervously.

"Is this…the same path we took the other day?" he asked, equal parts surprised and annoyed by the sudden tremble in his voice.

Ian nodded, and held up one hand, pausing to sigh before turning slowly around.

"What is it?" Cousins asked, seeing Ian's eyes focused behind them. "Oh," he answered himself, turning around as well to see the pair of rough-looking men following through the breezeway between the crops.

"A bit late for farming, eh?" Ian called out to them, but the only answer was a bit of derisive laughter from the smaller of the two men.

"Favo's employ, I'd wager," Cousins said.

Ian smiled wryly, "I wouldn't take that bet. One of the reasons I felt the Wilds would be best is precisely for this reason," he continued, softly enough for his words to reach only Cousins' ears, "much more unlikely to be unwittingly followed."

"I can see the allure," Cousins whispered back as the two large men approached.

One of the men was carrying a large smithing hammer, the other carried a pistol of some sort at his hip. Ian's breath hissed out between his teeth. "Have you still the Handle?" he asked Cousins softly.

"The handle – oh, that, yes. Why?"

"Get it out now," Ian instructed. "You'll need it."

Cousins reached into his shoulder bag and pulled out the curious piece of wood. It felt awkward and clumsy in his hand.

"You're holding it upside down," Ian said casually, reaching into his jacket.

The thugs broke into a dead run towards them, the larger one with the hammer raising it up by the handle and preparing to swing it down towards Ian.

Flipping it over in his hand, Cousins was forced to admit it did feel much better that way, though he suspected he'd feel better still if there were a blade attached to it.

"Here!" Ian said, grabbing Cousins by the right arm and raising it between them and the man with the hammer. Cousins felt a slight vibration in the wood, and suddenly a large frame of reinforced wood appeared – a shield, attached to the handle itself. The hammer slammed against it, but sent only the barest shiver down to Cousins' arm.

Ian pushed the shield abruptly, sending the man sprawling. The shield vanished, and Ian then drew Cousins back behind him with one arm while the other flicked a pair of hardened squares of paper in their direction.

"Close your eyes!" he hissed.

Too flustered by the activity to refuse the command, Cousins did as he was told, squinting his eyes tightly as a wave of heat turned the darkness into a shade of red, and then a tremendous explosion sent him reeling.

It felt as if he had wool shoved into his ears, and the loudest ringing he'd ever heard on top of that.

Hands grabbed at him, and it took him several moments of struggling before he realized it was Ian.

Ian dusted him off and held his face in his hands to look at his eyes. At about the time the ringing began to subside, Ian nodded his head and smiled. "Good lad," he said. "You're going to be just fine, now."

"Wha-" Cousins began, but a fit of coughing interrupted him. "What happened?" He glanced past Ian's shoulder to see a blackened area several meters wide, and still smoking. In the distance, a blue shimmer sparked to life; a great field of energy snapped into place around the entirety of Oldtown. "That's the Motive Wall," he observed. "That means it's…" his voice trailed off as he turned behind him into the deepening shadows.

"Sunset," Ian finished for him. "We should move quickly, the storm is coming."

"What storm?" Cousins asked. The sky had been clear just minutes earlier, but now, thick, dark clouds filled the air, and he could taste the coming rain on his lips.

"The storm I summoned to keep us safe and hide our tracks," he answered. Cousins could see a hint of something darker on Ian's face, nearly concealed by his usual smile.

"What is it, Ian," Cousins insisted. "There's something you're not telling me."

Ian's eyes returned briefly towards the city, and then again to Cousins. "I don't favor such a strong abuse of the Arts," he said. "I've set something in motion, and I fear for what might yet happen."

"Such as?" The winds were whipping up strongly now, forcing them to move on over the rock fence line and into the trees.

Quests & Answers

"That's the trouble, my lad," Ian replied, leading them through a winding maze of brush and overgrowth. "Nature prefers to move in a straight line. And when you push it," he added, drawing back a low-hanging branch to illustrate the point, "it tends to respond in kind." Releasing the branch, it whipped past them both with an impressive velocity. If Cousins had been standing in its path, it would have easily drawn blood.

They walked in silence for the next several minutes, finally arriving at what appeared in the storm's darkness to simply be a smooth hill cropping up from the mud. Cousins approached it, and struck his knuckles lightly against the rusted metal with a hollow clang.

"No more of that, young man," Ian cautioned. "There are many a beast out wandering these woods, we don't wish to alert them to an untimely end." He pointed up around to the far side of the structure. "Go wait in the shelter of its mouth, the insulation should keep you safe enough."

"Where will you be?"

Ian drew the collar of his jacket up over the long braid of his hair. "I have to go apologize to the storm for summoning it. Keep the girls safe until I arrive."

He stood, perplexed as the strange man walked off into the intensifying storm, and started as a lightning blast lit up the night sky. "Insulation should keep me safe enough? *Should*?!" In spite of his growing concerns, Cousins moved quickly around the Machine's half-buried head and crouched down to enjoy what brief dryness he could and tried not to imagine he was being eaten.

While he waited, he pulled the triangular box of marbles back out. He rolled the fire marble in between his thumb and forefinger, and nearly dropped it as it began to glow again. Probably not a good time, he thought urgently, but the tiny sphere only shone more brightly.

Movement outside the Machine's head caught his eye. Something small, and fast. He stood up, grabbed the Handle and hoped it would still work. *However it is that it works at all, that is*, he thought.

He kept the glowing marble behind him at first, so that its brightness didn't make him night-blind, but caught a solid glimpse of the figure ahead of him, and recognized the white hair beneath a slightly tattered parasol. Cousins tried to call out to her, but could barely hear himself over the torrents of rain that rattled against the ground and the metal shell of the Machine directly behind him.

At that moment, something caught her attention, and she spun around as another quickly-moving shape entered the clearing, Kari evidently; a realization which made him feel both warm and strangely uncomfortable. Before he had a chance to come to terms with that mystery, something altogether larger than all three of them combined leapt into the clearing.

With the light coming from behind him, he got a clear look at it. Though its hair was soaked and mud-matted, he could see its claws, teeth and curled horns glinting. Cousins noticed what had to be a pair of wings like a bat, folded down across its back.

The creature snarled, seemingly caught in the choice of finding its supper with either of the two girls. Rom took the lead, he noticed, making the decision for the beast. *Always a scrapper, that one*, he observed, *and never one to picture herself on the losing side of a fight.*

She tried to keep herself between the creature and Kari at all times, but the great range of its jumps proved it to be only a matter of time before it would achieve its desired positioning. Each time it leapt, Cousins thought for certain it had her; but she would dive, roll or even leap above it as it landed beneath her. It was too dark, even with the light from the marble, for Cousins to see with any detail. Lightning filled the clearing with flashes of illumination, but the darkness after it was gone felt even more disconcerting.

Rom and the beast made several passes, each time shocking Cousins with the girl's undeniably impressive skill at jumping; perhaps two or three times what a normal man could achieve, even in the best shape of his life. *Something odd about her; and not just her hair, to be certain.*

His mouth opened in warning, but if she heard him, she did not acknowledge it. The creature landed between the two girls and turned its attention on the easier meal. Rom responded by leaping up onto its back. It answered her move by unfurling its wings and bolting straight up into the storm-tossed sky.

Cousins heard his own panicked cry echoed by Kari. He rushed to her side, apologizing instantly for the fright his hand on her shoulder created. They had time for a moment's glance before the next bolt of lightning struck the sky directly overhead.

From somewhere over Cousins' right shoulder, Ian jumped past, skidding to a stop in the slick mud in front of them. He pointed at Cousins and yelled out for him to *get ready*, though Cousins wasn't sure exactly what he was to get ready for. Nevertheless, he gave Kari's shoulder a reassuring squeeze and moved a few steps closer until Ian, looking directly into the blackness overhead, held up a hand, palm forward.

In his other hand, he snapped two cards in half, generating a brief spark and puff of smoke which were instantly dissolved in the rain. His hands then shot straight above his head as a large object crashed down atop him. In the last meter before it landed, it seemed to slow, as if falling into a great and invisible pillow. After the shock of its appearance passed, Cousins could see that it was roughly the size and shape of the immense monster, but blackened and burnt, still sizzling with each drop of rain.

Ian grunted with the weight, but pointed his finger nearest the two children directly at Cousins, who instinctively held out his arms and caught the smoking body of his friend Rom.

Kari's scream behind him felt muffled, distant. All he could see was the burned skin and open, unblinking blue eyes as they stared up into a roiling sky.

The next hours were a blur. There had been a sort of reverence with which Ian had carried Rom's body back. He, meanwhile, had all but supported Kari as they returned through the Wild and the agricultural fields until they somehow arrived at the Apothecary. Ian had taken Rom's body in to Goya's parlor while Briseida stayed with Kari and Cousins. His eyes had remained on Kari most of the time they had waited. She had cried inconsolably for the first several hours, and had fallen asleep from exhaustion shortly before dawn.

At some point, there was a mug held in front of him. It contained something smelling of herbs wafting up in the steam to his nose. He glanced up to see Briseida there, her expression concerned and tired. She glanced meaningfully towards Kari, whose sleeping head was supported by one of the pillows Briseida had brought for them earlier. Though her eyes were closed, the lids were deeply reddened and, even in sleep, her breaths were heavy and tinged with sorrow.

Cousins couldn't think of anything he could say, and a faint shake of Briseida's head told him she didn't need him to. He took the offered cup and took a tentative sip of it. It made his lips tingle.

She nodded encouragingly for him to finish walking past him with a blanket held across her arm. Briseida carefully laid it atop Rom's slumbering friend, and paused as if to be certain the girl did not yet awaken.

The door into the salon behind her opened and Ian stepped out, his face a combination of sorrow and optimism.

"We'll know more soon," he whispered, eyeing Kari beside them. "All I can say for now is that all hope is not lost."

"Reaper's breath," Cousins swore softly. "I thought... well, I thought she was gone for certain."

Briseida looked quickly at Ian, who answered her unspoken expression with a wink. "No, my young friend, there is something you should see."

Confused, Cousins looked back to Kari. Briseida touched his shoulder, "She'll be fine, I will sit with her until you return."

He got up, stretched his back and glanced once more at Kari before following Ian back into the salon.

The salon looked like a dining room, but with all the chairs lined up at the walls as opposed to at the long table in the center of the room. At one end stood perhaps the oldest woman Cousins had ever seen, though the commanding expression of resolve etched upon her face made her seem somehow younger than Ian. Her hands rested, palms down, atop the table. Rom lay atop the table, a single white sheet having been laid across her from the neck down. It took him several more moments to both realize, and then believe, that the sheet was moving.

Cousins gasped, in spite of himself.

Ian closed the door behind them.

The old woman nodded her head. "Look closely, boy," she said, gesturing towards Rom.

He was comfortable in admitting it was perhaps the last thing he should have wanted to look at, but he did as bidden, his reluctance replaced almost instantly with incredulity.

Cousins stepped forward; one step, two, and then moved the rest of the way to the table.

"But this isn't possible!" he said, uncertain of exactly why he was still whispering.

Ian walked around to stand on the opposite side of the table from Cousins. He said nothing, but simply nodded as if to confirm that it, in fact, *was* possible.

"Ian, I caught her when she fell. She wasn't breathing!"

Nodding patiently, Ian extended a hand towards the old woman. "Cousins, this is Goya Parva; she is an old friend of mine, and an impressive healer."

She waved off the compliment as if it were an annoying fly. "I can't take credit in this case, of course," she said. Her voice was soft but seemed to carry all the way into his ears. "She's doing all the work, I'm just keeping her fed and hydrated."

Rom's white hair was fully grown back, brushed back from her face. And the skin of her face was unblemished, pale and slightly freckled as always. But what truly drew his attention was in the very center of her forehead. There, beneath the skin and roughly the size of his fingernail, was a purplish glow, shining faintly. It didn't look so much like a lump or a bruise, but flat and faceted like a sizeable gem.

His thoughts flashed back to his studies as a small child, and the random bits of information gathered through his life. The *jeweled skin* was a feature only mentioned in the old tomes of knowledge, or in the few remaining paintings or sculptures that could be found around Oldtown. It was a singular descriptive, always in reference to a single entity, one he had thought long lost to tradition and myth.

The blood pounded in his ears.

"Reaper's breath!" he whispered.

Ian's eyes sparkled as he nodded in confirmation. "Though, in all fairness to her, lad, you may wish a different epithet going forward."

"You mean…" Cousins reached out to the table for support.

Goya shook her head. "It is not yet fixed in the stars, both of you. No matter what path she is choosing, her choice will either be made by her or for her. Let our little snow angel find her way back and then we shall see." Looking back to Ian, she pointed a gnarled finger at him. "The Matrons will be worried at their empty beds," she said, scarcely hiding a grimace at speaking of the philosophical order who ran the orphanage that cared for Rom, Kari and dozens more children, "See that she is returned safely. Let what transpires do so in the place she has come to call her home. Take the children with you, and explain to the boy here what other favors we must ask of him."

Leading the stunned Cousins from the room, Goya walked him to the door and pointed towards the stirring Kari. "She will want to remain by Romany's side, and that would be well. I'm sure the girl will want a friendly face to see when she awakens."

"But," he sputtered, confused, "how is this even possible?"

But Goya merely smiled. "More is possible than you have yet to imagine, boy. Now, go help your friend get ready to go back while Briseida and I take care of other matters."

Briseida rose and stepped past him and Cousins knelt beside Kari, reaching a single hand towards her to rouse her. He wanted to touch her hair for some reason, though it was caked with flecks of mud and leaves from her mad run through the Wild last night. Her eyes fluttered open to see him paused there, hand outstretched.

"Oh, I…" he began, but couldn't think of any of his right words, as they had clearly abandoned him for a more eloquent master. "Rom's okay," he whispered. "She's still sleeping, but… I don't know how, but she's fine."

She bolted to her feet. "Where is she? Can I see her?"

He stood between her and the door. "Ian's bringing her out and we're going to take her back to the Orphanage."

Somehow, he managed to keep her relatively calm until the door opened and Ian stepped out, carrying the unconscious Rom in his arms. If Kari noticed the two women at the doorway, she made no indication; her attention was fixed entirely upon her friend.

He held the door open for Ian and Kari, and they made their way from the corner shop, walking east towards the Orphanage that sat near the base of the Wall. Ahead of them, it loomed across the skyline, white and featureless, sweeping up towards the sky as a constant reminder of their ancestors' exile.

Cousins paused as a brief spell of dizziness passed him; his vision blurred momentarily, and, just for a moment, his eyes played tricks on him. For just a second, it had looked as if the Wall was gone; that only an unending blue sky met the far horizon. He shook his head, and caught up with Ian and Kari as they took Rom back to the dormitories.

Something's happened to the world, Cousins thought. *It's different than it was yesterday, and it's going to be different again tomorrow. All that was, need not be again,* strange, half-remembered words fluttering past his memory. He took a deep breath and adjusted the bag over his shoulder.

Well, he thought, *if it's going to be a new world, then I need to start learning a fair deal more about the one I'm already living in.* He pondered that idea as they walked. *Beginning with Art*, he decided, nodding in satisfaction at the idea. *Yes. It's time Cousins gave in and started learning that.*

His eyes moved between the Wall and the girl who walked only a few paces ahead of him. The pain and anguish of last night was already fading from her face, and the hopeful smile she now wore looked to him like the sunrise after a storm. He sighed softly.

Maybe Art won't be the only thing about my life to change, he told himself. And in spite of the fears that realization might have otherwise caused him, this was like no other day. Today, the thought made him smile.

BONUS MATERIALS

Akhet

Book One of "Sekhmet's Light"

By H. L. Reasby

Chapter 1

With her oxygen mask in securely in place over her nose and mouth, Dr. Nicole Salem descended below ground level, the rope slowly sliding through the descender at the front of her harness. "Speed's good, Marcus," she said into the mask.

"See anything yet?" Marcus' voice crackled through the earpiece, loud and clear. She knew that he must be riveted to the screen displaying the feed from the small video camera attached to her helmet. As their 'tech wrangler', Marcus was very protective of their gear; almost as protective as he was of his girlfriend, Nicole, herself.

"Not yet. The stone making up the roof is very thick... and is definitely dressed stone. I can make out the joins between the sandstone blocks. It also looks like it might be deeper than we thought," Nicole said, turning her head to pan the camera about.

"Understood, but keep in contact," the voice of her former teacher and mentor, Dr. Alex Hodges, advised this time.

"Right," Nicole said, frowning as she dropped below the roof stones. The chamber was at least a hundred yards across and its length lost beyond the edge of her high-intensity light, but there was a distinct lack of decoration that was struck her as odd. The sandstone was dark gold where her light touched it, evocative of the dunes above her head, and she could, again, see the lines between the blocks making up the chamber that told her clearly that this was no natural formation.

"This is bizarre." Nicole trailed off in a softer voice, her mind working through the possibilities of how the structure came to be built like it was. "There's no statuary, no glyphs that I can see from here. I'm sure that it extends beyond the range of my light to the northeast." She added with an undisguised hint of excitement in her voice.

She reached up and touched the earpiece. She could hear crackling and a hint of what must have been Marcus' voice, but she couldn't make out any of the words. "Say again, Marcus, I'm not making that out." There was a series of hisses and pops, but not a hint of a voice in the transmission this time. She gave a surprised gasp as the rope suddenly jerked upward. Marcus must have reversed the winch to pull her up when he stopped being able to hear her.

Nicole swept the light around, trying to get a better look at the walls and floor. She realized she could see the floor, a smooth sandy surface some thirty feet below her, and thought she could see pictures on the walls, though whether they were hieroglyphs, hieratic, or some other form of writing, she couldn't be certain. "Marcus, stop!" she said, trying to get the upward motion to halt, but her signal apparently wasn't getting through any better than Marcus' was. "Damn it," she growled, the harness jangling softly as she started feeding rope through the descender again to counter the upward movement.

Just as she was thinking about how she was going to tell both Marcus and Hodges off for the interruption, the rope jerked again: downward this time.

"What the hell?" She looked up toward the sunlight above. "What are they doing up there?" There were a couple more sharp downward jerks that sent her equipment rattling again and then fear started to creep in. "Maybe the winch is broken?" she mused to herself, peering upward again. "Marcus was right; we should've gotten a new one instead of trusting this one."

The words had barely left her lips before the rope went slack and she was in freefall. So startled, she didn't even have the opportunity to scream, Nicole plummeted into the dark below her. The scream started to come, and then the wind was driven from her lungs by the sharp impact of her back meeting the sandy floor.

She lay there stunned in the midst of a cloud of dust for a couple of minutes, gasping the air back into her lungs with harsh coughs, before she realized that the chamber was now filled with light.

"Easy, khered, breathe easy," a soft voice murmured, stroking the end of her ponytail back away from her face and deftly removing the oxygen mask. It took her a moment to realize that the voice wasn't speaking English. The language was strange and familiar at the same time, warm and fluid, yet fierce.

After a moment, her eyes focused once more and she found herself staring up at a woman of around forty with dark skin and thick black hair that hung around her face in a series of braids woven with strands of colored fabric. Her clothing was simple, a traditional linen Egyptian kilt which wrapped around the hips, and was dyed red, and a matching wrap around her torso which covered her breasts and twisted up to secure the garment behind her neck. Despite her age, her body was trim and well-muscled enough to be the envy of a women half her age.

"Where am I?" Nicole asked, pushing up onto her elbows.

The woman smiled and rose to her feet, offering Nicole her hand.

Nicole took the hand and found herself pulled to her feet with surprising ease by the smaller woman. It was then that she fully registered the clothing and the sword at the woman's hip. "Who are you? What's going on here?"

The woman laughed the sound an unrestrained chortle that brought an instinctive smile to Nicole's face for a moment. "I am Meshrew," she said, grinning up at Nicole who stood a good eight inches taller than her, the expression softening her brown eyes.

"I am the eldest priestess here and am responsible for preparing you." The woman's voice was deep and slightly husky, colored with a gentle humor that made Nicole wonder if there was some joke here that she was missing.

"Meshrew," Nicole said, looking around. Evening, her mind translated. The walls were now thickly covered with hieroglyphs that she would have liked to take a moment to study, but Meshrew didn't give her a chance.

"Yes, 'evening'," The smaller woman said, seeming to read Nicole's thoughts. "My parents were somewhat lacking in imagination for what to name me, though, I suppose, that is understandable when you are the last of ten children. I was born just after Ra's barque descended on its nightly journey through the underworld, so I became 'Meshrew'." The woman's voice was warm and soothing, but there was an aura of command about her that made the light pressure of a hand against the small of Nicole's back into an undeniable demand.

Nicole smiled. "It's a beautiful name," she murmured, allowing herself to be swept forward. She looked down and realized that the rope that had been her lifeline to the world above had been cleanly severed about a foot away from the carabineer it was attached to.

"Thank you. Now come. There is much to do," Meshrew said, her tone very businesslike as she waved a trio of younger women over, the oldest of which looked as though she were barely out of her teens. All of them were dressed similarly to Meshrew, though their clothing was of pale blue linen rather than red, and while none of them wore a sword, as Meshrew did, each carried a long slightly curved dagger that could nearly pass for a short sword. "Prepare her."

Nicole found herself passed off to the three who immediately began to escort her off. "Wait! What am I preparing for?" she called after Meshrew, but got no reply. She started to pull free of the group guiding her, but stopped when she got a look at some of the glyphs near the doorway they were headed toward. The hieroglyphs depicted the tale of Sekhmet's birth. The sun Ra became angry with humanity for turning their backs on him and ignoring the gifts he has given them. In his rage, he ripped out his own eye and cast it to Earth where it became a fiery goddess whom he called Sekhmet. She went on a rampage to avenge her father's name and all but wiped out humanity before Ra saw that she had no intention of stopping. He realized that without humanity, there would be little reason for him and the other gods to exist.

Ra was able to trick Sekhmet into stopping by flooding a vast plain with beer that he dyed red so that she would believe it to be blood. She drank down the beer and became so intoxicated that she passed out. When she woke, Ra convinced her to stop the slaughter. Later, at her father's urging, Sekhmet created a champion to guide and protect the Pharaoh and the kingdoms from their enemies.

Nicole tried to stop her forward movement so that she could study the pictures more closely, but the women were implacable and herded her through the doorway without slowing their pace. This time, however, her astonishment was sufficient to stop Nicole dead in her tracks. She barely even noticed when the last of the trio bumped into her from behind, before realizing that Nicole had halted.

The chamber she found herself in was significantly smaller than the one she had left, though far more sumptuous. It was more brightly lit with braziers spaced around the walls and several at the edges of the long, narrow pool in the center of the floor, allowing Nicole to see the space more clearly. The smell of the water from the pool was alluring after the dry sterility of the desert above, particularly when combined with the smoky fragrance of whatever it was they were using for fuel in the braziers.

There were pillows scattered between the walls and the pool's perimeter and the walls were painted with murals of life along the Nile with all its beauty (shown in the lotus blossoms and smiling faces of the people as they fished, gathered papyrus, and performed other activities of daily life) and dangers (crocodiles sunning themselves on the shores near where women washed clothes and bathed, and hippos cavorting near barques moving along the river, forcing the pilots to keep a wary eye out). She only got a cursory look at the pictures before she realized that she was subject to a piercing amber gaze.

Barely five yards away from her stood a lioness and her three cubs, the adult regarding her with an assessing air that caused the hairs at the nape of her neck to rise as Nicole realized that the animal could easily deem her prey. The women seemed unconcerned by the predator's presence and, after a flick of an ear, the lioness seemed to dismiss her entirely, pulling one cub into the circle of her front paws to bathe it.

After a moment, the tallest of the three young women she took Nicole's arm once more, holding her firmly as the girls surrounded her on all sides. Expertly, they stripped Nicole's equipment from her, then starting on her clothing. "You must be cleansed before we can allow you before the goddess," the leader of the trio explained.

"Goddess? What goddess?" she asked, trying to push their hands away. "I don't understand what's going on here. Stop!" Even with her resistance, first trying to bat their hands away, then trying to turn back toward the entrance through which she came, and even throwing a punch at one of them, which was casually dodged, it was only a matter of moments before her clothing had been tossed aside into a pile. Two of the women took her hands firmly and tugged her toward the pool.

"Let go of me!" Nicole demanded as she was pulled into the blessedly cool water. The bottom sloped down to about four feet deep; the illusion of greater depth was achieved by painting the stone floor of the pool black. Despite herself, sigh of pleasure escaped Nicole's lips, her desert-parched body relishing the coolness of the water enveloping her. She had almost forgotten how nice it was to be able to submerge herself in water to bathe; a couple of months of sponge baths made it necessary to forget, otherwise, the feeling of 'ickiness' would never go away.

It was a truly bizarre experience for Nicole as the pair of young women who accompanied her into the water bathed her and washed her hair, but it also felt right somehow. The two were clearly very accustomed to this sort of thing and it showed as they combined a soothing massage into the washing of her hair. To her bemusement, Nicole found herself relaxing and actually enjoying their attention as the grime and sweat that was a natural side effect of working in the desert was cleansed.

Once she was clean, Nicole ascended the slope on the other side of the pool, water streaming from her body. In the cool air of the bath chamber, she found herself shivering slightly which was a very pleasant change from the scorching heat above ground.

Meshrew stood a few feet from the edge of the pool with an assortment of items, waiting for her. Meshrew watched Nicole emerge, her expression serious, verging on sternness now as she examined the young Westerner.

The young women who had accompanied her into the water wrapped thick, absorbent linen around her hips and applied firm, but gentle pressure to her shoulders to encourage her to kneel in front of the older woman. The feelings of confusion and unease that had faded in the bath disappeared entirely as she looked up at Meshrew. She felt that she belonged here now though her logical mind told her that the idea was ridiculous, that she belonged up above with Marcus and the others, and that this was all too strange for her to accept. Meshrew's smile down at her appeared pleased.

There were no further words as Nicole settled back on her haunches. The young women gathered around behind her and each began plaiting sections of her long hair into thin braids woven with strips of white, gold, red, and blue fabric which would mingle with the rest of her hair which was left loose. Meshrew, in the meantime, picked up one of several small ceramic pots beside her and began applying the oils and paints inside them to Nicole's skin, drawing the eye of Ra, the sun disc, and several other symbols that Nicole either couldn't see or didn't immediately recognize.

She didn't know how long she knelt there while the women worked, but when they were finished, Meshrew motioned Nicole to her feet. "You shall not be touched again until you have emerged. Come." It wasn't a request and Nicole pushed herself to her feet, allowing the absorbent linen to fall around her feet.

The sense of belonging here intensified as she approached another portal, this one blocked from the bathing chamber by a teak wood door with a symbol embossed on it: a golden silouhette of Sekhmet in profile with the sun disk ascendant above her in blood red with a black cobra draped over the top so that its head was suspended above Sekhmet's. "Through there?"

Meshrew nodded. "Yes. Do not worry. We will be waiting for you," she murmured, and then pointed to the door. "Go."

Nicole hesitated a moment. The glyph on the door was strangely familiar; something about it resonated in her heart in a way that was more powerful than mere déjà vu. It was like the memory of a cherished dream from childhood which had been long forgotten in the cynicism and routine of adult life.

She nodded to herself, and then walked toward the door. When she was five feet away, the door swung inward, with a squeak of protest from long unused hinges, to allow her entrance. Although her conscious mind was surprised to see that no one was operating the door, deep down she realized didn't seem strange at all that the ancient portal functioned on its own.

The room she entered was cool and darker than the antechamber she'd left, lit only by a few braziers in the corners and a pair flanking the centerpiece of the room: standing a full twenty feet high was a gold statue of Sekhmet the Destroyer. It was the goddess'

hybrid form that of a young woman with the head of a lioness, the sun disc ascendant above her.

The red of her gown and the sun, as well as the detailing of the face were enameled on the gold to give it a realistic appearance. The arms of the statue were crossed in front of her, the right hand holding a khopesh sword, with its distinctive shape which vaguely resembled a sickle joined sword base, which extended up past her left shoulder, the left hand holding an ankh, the Egyptian symbol of life, which came up over her right shoulder. The beauty of the statue brought prickling, unshed tears of pleasure to Nicole's eyes as she gazed upon it, taking a few seconds to appreciate the craftsmanship before stepping further into the room.

There was a dais in front of the statue, which Nicole walked to and knelt upon. She bowed her head, her hands resting lightly on her thighs, and waited. Somehow she knew that if she were supposed to say anything, to invoke the goddess in some way, she would have known to do so, but she said nothing.

Nicole sat there for a long time, how long she couldn't know. She sat there until the muscles of her legs started to protest the lack of movement, until the room seemed to grow warmer and the light from the braziers intensified. Nicole lifted her head and found herself looking up into the face of the goddess, caught in the molten gold of her divine gaze. The metal head, now as flexible as flesh, tilted and a small smile curled the corners of the goddess' lips enough to show the tips of her upper canine teeth.

"Hello, khered." 'Hello, my child,' her mind translated automatically. The voice was huge and she could almost feel the dais shaking beneath her knees, but also warm and soothing with a purring quality to it that eased the last of her nervousness. "I was beginning to think that you had forgotten me."

Nicole bowed from the waist so that her forehead rested atop her hands on the stone. "Only in my mind, mewet nefer; my heart has always remembered."

Sekhmet chuckled softly and a gentle touch on Nicole's shoulder prompted her to sit up. "You are, of course, forgiven, khered. You found your way home when you were ready to, when your spirit was ready for the work to be done."

Nicole smiled up at the goddess, reveling in the acceptance and implied praise. "I am ready to do as you bid, Mother."

Sekhmet smiled, exposing enough gleaming white teeth to have spooked most people; her canines were about as long as Nicole's arm. "I know that you are, child. I wish I could give you more time to prepare for the charge I am to place upon your shoulders, but you would not have been drawn here were you not strong enough already."

Nicole felt if her heart swelled with any more pride it would burst, temporarily overshadowing her doubts and concerns. "I pray I will prove myself worthy of your attentions, Mother." She bowed again then found one of the goddess' massive hands taking hold of her chin in a tender, but irresistible grip.

"Stand, Nicole Salem," Sekhmet bid her, keeping hold of Nicole's jaw as she obeyed. "You will remember what you need, as you need it. Your mind is modern, though your

heart is true, and I would not cause you the distress that granting you your full birthright immediately would cause."

"Will I remember this?" The thought of losing the knowledge of the goddess' face caused Nicole the first tremor of fear she'd had since entering the sacred pool.

Sekhmet smiled. "You will remember, though it will seem as a dream at first. Do not worry, Nicole. My hand and my eye will be upon you, though lightly. If you need me, we will meet as you dream." She tilted her head, her eyes warm and affectionate. "It is easiest that way as my powers have waned in these less enlightened times."

Nicole nodded. "I understand," she said, her confidence returning.

"Now then." Sekhmet moved her hand from Nicole's jaw and touched her fingertips to the Nicole's brow. As the warm metal contacted her skin, Nicole's back bowed and every muscle in her body drew taught. The pain was intense, arching her back and locking her jaws open in a scream which never made it past her throat, a scream that seemed to go on forever and when it was over she collapsed onto her back on the dais her eyes transfixed as they lay on the once more inanimate statue above her until consciousness faded.

To be continued in *Akhet, book one of the* *Sekhmet's Light trilogy.*

Awaken

The Children of Divinity, Book One

By Garth Reasby

Chapter 1

T he bitter cold of the Afghani night had yet to give way to the oppressive heat of the day and the sun had not even begun its slow crawl from behind the rugged mountains. The terrain was treacherous at best, though the combination of sharp, uneven rock, prolific scrub brush and several large camel thorn trees provided excellent protection for the small village nestled near the steep rock wall. The rickety collection of patchwork buildings had been built near where an uneven smuggler's pass exited so that travelers could rest there after making the long journey from Pakistan.

In the quiet pre-dawn, the sound of two vehicles approaching echoed off the tall rock walls that rimmed the valley where the unnamed village sat. The sputtering cough-like echo of each truck's four cylinder gas engine created enough of a racket to stir the one dog of the village and send him into a fit of sharp barking. The barking ended in a yelp of pain when a weary sentry kicked the dog into silence.

"Stupid cur. My wife complains enough even when she's slept all night. That damned dog and its incessant barking!" Dehqan cursed in Pashto while he and a fellow Mujahedeen picked their way through the uneven terrain along the ridgeline on their way back to the village which was over a kilometer away.

The other man grinned widely with a mouth full of nicotine-stained teeth. "Your wife will be cranky again my friend, and no doubt twice as ugly without more sleep."

Dehqan glanced at his friend Babur and chuckled quietly at the joke. "Yes, but not so ugly as your own with twice again as much rest." Both men allowed their amusement to fade into silence as they continued down the rough slope towards their homes.

The sounds of the two sentries' battered Russian combat boots crunching on the rocks disappeared as they wound their way down the broken trail. Neither man noticed the concealed form that lay on the ground not more than five meters away from the trail where they had traded barbs. The form remained motionless until the scent of sweat, clove cigarettes, and gun oil the two men reeked of faded. Even then there was no obvious motion from the shadowy shape that blended seamlessly with the straw colored halfa grass where it lurked. Hidden by a shaggy ghille suit carefully crafted from the local foliage, the distinctly feminine form was rendered nearly invisible even in the full light of day. Here in the dim pre-dawn she was a ghost.

It had been so for two days and nights. Thankfully, the straw colored ghille suit combined with the lose-fitting British lightweight DPM fatigues, or battle dress utilities and the Underarmor thermals beneath provided some protection from the frigid cold of the Afghani nights. Those same layers also kept the blistering sun from the woman's skin. Though it was better than being fully exposed to the intense sunlight that baked the countryside, she found it insufferably warm. Still, the ghille suit did what it was designed to do and reduced the chance that someone would detect the sniper wearing it.

The trucks were closer now, perhaps three kilometers from the woman's position. It was the same two beaten and battered Toyota T-100 pickup trucks, one red, and the other blue. Both vehicles were packed with Taliban fighters. They were carrying all manner of weaponry from old Soviet AK-47 assault rifles to World War Two era bolt action rifles. The woman that was concealed beneath the camouflage narrowed her eyes and continued her vigil. She had counted roughly twenty fighters in the village in addition to the fifteen that went out in the trucks nightly. She had been in the middle of the snake's nest for two days' time, but that didn't bother the young woman from Northampton. She was there because she was the only one who could make it so deep into enemy territory without being discovered.

Pushing the brief moment of reflection to the back of her mind, like the worry before it, Jordan focused her attention on the mission at hand. Fate seemed inclined to reward her discipline. The procession of twenty men and donkeys Jordan had been waiting for picked their way out of a large shadowed crack in the weathered rock wall as if on cue. The first hints of dawn caressed the stone wall's weather-beaten surface as the group of insurgents navigated the rough and uneven terrain of the old smuggler's path. They seemed oblivious to the danger they were in and made casual conversation as they walked.

Jordan carefully adjusted the aim of her Accuracy International L115A3 Arctic Warfare Super Magnum sniper rifle and centered the cross hairs of its Schmidt & Bender 3-12X variable scope on the center of the lead walker's face. *Not him*, she thought.

The sleek L115A3 was a highly accurate bolt action rifle that had a polymer stock and an adjustable cheek rest so that each shooter could set the weapon to their own tastes. The stock was cast in a khaki tan while the metal barrel and bipod were painted in a simple, but effective, desert camouflage to match. The long scope that was mounted just in front of the bolt was also painted to blend in with the terrain. To reduce the chance of detection, the optic had been fitted with honeycomb shaped anti-reflection devices. Though different versions of the rifle were designed to use a variety of calibers, Jordan's super magnum was chambered for .338 Lapua. Thanks to this large-caliber high-performance round, the L115A3 was capable of taking down any game animal, including an elephant, which meant that any human struck by a well-aimed bullet was unlikely to live. The L115A3 rifle was a precision instrument, a surgeon's scalpel in the world of warfare, and perfect for a master marksman like Jordan. The weapon was practical, reliable, accurate, but, most of all, it reminded Jordan of her father, himself a former sniper. She knew it would never let her down.

Continuing to seek out her target, Jordan repeated the adjustment eight times before she saw the familiar features of the target. She knew his name, though she didn't dwell on it. He was the target and that was it. It didn't matter what he was called. His distinctive features were what were important, features that he had just revealed by unwrapping the off-white cloth from around his head to allow the rising sun to warm his face. The man had helped orchestrate over two dozen attacks against American and British forces in Afghanistan, and had been responsible for a terrorist bombing at Heathrow airport only four hours after the destruction of the Twin Towers. He had murdered hundreds, but worse yet, he had trained hundreds more, a cadre of like-minded fanatics that could potentially kill thousands, of innocent people. Jordan was here to make sure he had trained his last terrorist, committed his last murder.

A strong, cold wind caught the cloth about the man's head and tugged it to the side causing Jordan to smile slightly. The flapping of the material allowed her to easily gauge the wind speed where he was standing. She waited for the group to make their way down the trail towards the Taliban-controlled village that was their destination and, more importantly, past the areas she had already pre-ranged so she didn't need a spotter to assist her. At just over two thousand eight hundred meters in poor light and high, inconsistent wind, it was a tough shot at best. For most snipers, it wasn't possible. It was why she had come.

Jordan clicked off two ticks of the windage adjustment knob on her scope and let her finger lightly caress the trigger of her rifle, releasing her breath in a long, slow exhalation. The target continued along unsuspectingly, one step, another, and then another. The man continued to talk with his companions, Jordan's eyes watched his face through the magnified optics of her scope while her breath trickled from her parted lips. Her mind focused on a span of time between breaths and everything in the world around her slowed down.

Unexpectedly, the Mujahedeen leader's head started to turn to face Jordan's position. The man's eyes met Jordan's through the view of her scope and began to shift from a warm brown to solid white. Like the scrabbling of dozens of clawed feet on stone, an unintelligible whisper filled Jordan's mind. A pain so intense that it made Jordan's jaw clench accompanied the disturbing sound and seemed to be growing. Instinctively, Jordan squeezed the trigger. The familiar recoil of the weapon rippled through her arms and shoulders, but she kept the rifle on target.

The bullet crossed the intervening terrain quickly, leaving a hint of distorted air in its passing. It crossed over the tops of several bushes, through the Y shaped intersection of branches on a camel thorn tree, then rushed through a fist sized space between two large boulders. Unerringly, the projectile continued on its path for just over two seconds before it sped past another man's ear and struck the target in the left eye.

The .338 Lapua round had lost much of its kinetic energy on its long journey but it still struck the terrorist leader like a sledgehammer. Just before the bullet struck, the man smiled serenely at Jordan, the whispering in her head coalescing into a single phrase, *"Allahu akbar."*

The force of the impact was such that the target's head barely moved but the back of it explosively sprayed on the large boulder he was walking by. His companions immediately hit the ground and started shouting loudly. The village came alive with activity as the report from the large bore rifle reached them and shook the guerilla fighters from their sleep.

Soon people were streaming from nearly every ramshackle structure, yelling for everyone to prepare for attack. Even the previously silenced dog was barking again as people rushed about in a panic. The remaining nineteen men in the procession opened fire with their Russian-made Kalashnikov AK-47 assault rifles. Most of the insurgents fired into the areas that they thought the attacker was in, which resulted in several of the fighters firing in different directions. Only a couple of the disorganized men managed to bring fire in Jordan's direction though none of the hastily fired bullets reached her.

Though her shot was well over the world record for a long range kill, Jordan took no time to revel in it. It wasn't the first she had made at such a range. None of her best shots would ever be recorded in a history book, yet history had been irrevocably altered by many of them. Jordan took no pleasure in killing, but understood that there were certain people that couldn't be dealt with by any other means.

Jordan was all business as she put her rifle in the long tan sniper drag bag next to her and rolled up the shooting mat she had spent the last two days on. Tucking that away, she thrust her hand into a pouch and pushed herself into a crouch holding a small bottle in her hand. With a flick of her thumb, Jordan opened and then dumped the small container of vinegar she had retrieved over the entire area where she was laying. The strong-smelling liquid would prevent any dogs from tracking her by scent. With practiced efficiency she slung the drag bag over her shoulder and grabbed the

Heckler and Koch G-36K assault rifle from where it lay next to her.

The sudden and unexpected sound of a boot grinding stones together made Jordan freeze in place. Turning her head, the British operative stared into the eyes of the Afghani man, imaging herself as thin and light as a morning's breeze.

Dehqan shook his head and lowered his battered AK-47 assault rifle, his eyes squinting in the haze of the rapidly arriving dawn. Cautiously, he walked forward and wrinkled his nose, the harsh scent of vinegar unpleasant and unwelcome, though he could just barely make out the fading scent of burned gunpowder. The Afghani fighter could have sworn he's seen someone several meters down the trail. A woman. A tall woman with dark hair half hidden by a backwards-turned tan baseball cap and a curtain of local plant life pushed back from a camouflaged face. She had the most intense and beautiful blue eyes he had ever seen, but suddenly she was gone as if she had never been there. Dehqan blinked rapidly as if the act would bring the woman back into existence, but she did not return. A voice from behind called his name and the poppy farmer turned 'freedom fighter' jumped.

"Dehqan what is it? What did you see?" Babur rasped quietly in Pashto.

"Nothing…nothing, just a trick of the morning light."

******

Quests & Answers

It had been over ninety minutes since Jordan eliminated her target. Since then she had kept up a steady run through the rocks. The remaining insurgents had set out to try and find the person responsible for killing their leader, but Jordan pushed on hard and fast to out-distance them. She made her way into another hilly area dotted with large rocks and small caves. Jordan had anticipated that she may have hard time getting out of the area when she originally designed the mission, so she spent several days locating places she could hide as well as store equipment.

As she approached one of her caches Jordan heard a faint metallic rattling off in the distance. About a kilometer off, one of the battered Toyota pickups sped down the dusty road packed with Taliban fighters. Its engine sputtered in protest as the driver pushed it far beyond what the poorly-maintained machine could handle. Surprisingly, the engine held and the dust covered machine sped past Jordan's position, leaving a wake of black exhaust in the air behind it.

Jordan watched the truck pass from where she crouched in the rocks and remained completely motionless. After it was gone, she turned and ducked into a crack in the wall behind her. She knew that the guerillas would most likely drive until they thought they were well ahead of her and make their way back on foot.

They're a tenacious lot, I'll give them that, Jordan thought as she moved into the small passage in a half crouch.

Once she was a meter inside the passage, Jordan pulled a small tan box from her combat vest and placed it at the mouth of the cave amongst a small pile of rocks. She flipped a small toggle switch on the side of the device and then moved further into what was little more than a water carved pocket. The cave was only four meters deep, a meter wide and maybe a meter and a half tall with fairly smooth surfaces. During a good rain, the water would rush in through a small hole in ceiling and out of the crack in the wall. Jordan moved to the back of the shallow cave and pulled an assortment of brush off of the cache of supplies she had hidden several days prior.

The waiting three-day pack was tan and loaded with ammunition for the G36K, as well as Jordan's semi-automatic .45 caliber pistol. In addition, it had six L-2A2 fragmentation grenades and four N-110 smoke grenades that were divided into different colors. One was red and one was green and they were to be used for signaling, the other two were standard grey smoke for creating concealment. Most importantly, the pack had full hydration bladder for Jordan's Camelbak water carrier which she opened and took a long drink from.

After letting the semi-cool water run down her throat, Jordan exhaled long and slow to ease some of the tension from her body. She had pushed hard to get to the small refuge using short bursts of speed followed by minutes of hiding to leap frog from cover to cover in order to stay ahead of any foot pursuit. Jordan secured the top on the new bladder and swapped out the old for the new, placing the spent rubber bladder in her pack.

I should have waited and blown the engine blocks on the two trucks to put them all on foot. Rookie mistake, girl, you should have tidied up that bit before you exfiltrated, Jordan chided herself and pulled her ghille suit off. She rolled the sections of it and strapped the bundle to her three-day pack just in case she needed it again. It was no substitute for her gifts but they were hard to use at a full run, especially against large numbers of people.

The purpose for taking the camouflage suit with her was twofold. She wasn't going to leave a trail for the Taliban fighters to follow, or anything with her DNA on it. No trail of bread crumbs for anyone to follow back to who she was or who she worked for.

Jordan reached into the pack and pulled out a high-calorie concentrate bar she had wrapped in a piece of aluminum foil. These weren't standard-issue ration, but Jordan needed the extra calories after three days of relatively little to eat and the brief but high level of energy she expended in her retreat. The candy bar-sized was pasty white and looked like hard taffy though it tasted like very bland oatmeal. Jordan unwrapped one side of the calorie bar before she popped the end of it in her mouth to let her saliva soften it up.

As she worked at consuming the small bar, Jordan reflected on the past three months since her assignment to work with 22 SAS's A Squadron. Jordan's director, Nigel Stevens, had never admitted it while she was in the room, but Jordan was one of his few operatives that could make it so far into enemy territory without being detected. Her past work had shown she was exceptionally good at getting into, and out of, locations that were so-called impossible targets. Jordan knew that Stevens' real issue was that he couldn't figure out how she did it. It was her secret and she was going to keep it as long as possible.

The first month of the assignment had been training with the SAS team so that Jordan would know how to work with them without the need for excessive communication. It was a lot of move and cover exercises, night exercises, and kill house drills at Credenhill. The men had treated her with mild courtesy and professionalism, however, they pushed her. At the time, Jordan wasn't sure if it was because she was a woman, or if they just wanted to test her ability to keep up with them. She had played both games before. In the male-dominated field of work, a woman had to show they were just as skilled as the men and twice as tough. They had done their best to make her quit, mixing misogynist humor in with the grueling training. Jordan was *no* quitter. In fact, they learned that she was every bit the marksman that she was made out to be and that she was as strong and as fast as any of the men. By the time that month was out, she had convinced them that she could keep up and more.

Once the team had made it in country, they immediately set out to locate their target. It had taken nearly two months to find out about the small, unnamed village that was arguably within the Afghan border. They quickly realized that they would have to go in to get their target as an airstrike would kill civilians as well as the fighters. Despite what the media portrayed, they weren't there to murder innocents. After numerous simulations, Jordan knew that the entire team of eight would never be able to make it so far in and get out alive. Even though it had earned her no friends, Jordan made the decision to go in alone, keeping the team on standby in case she needed help during extraction.

A crackle and hiss in Jordan's left ear brought her out of memory and back to the present. The familiar voice of A Squadron's commanding officer, Paul Killian, was strong and clear over the small ear piece

Jordan wore. "Cobra One-Five to Viper Zero-Two-Two. Come in, over."

Jordan brought the thumb and index finger of her hand to the activator studs of her throat microphone to open the channel. "Viper Zero-Two-Two, here."

The voice that came over the communications net was professional and to the point. "Viper Zero-Two-Two, status."

"In process of exfil to point Bravo," Jordan replied and glanced at the black dive watch on her left wrist. She quickly estimated how long it would take her to get to the rally point where the SAS team waited for her. "ETA ninety minutes. Be advised that tangos are agitated and on the prowl."

"Confirm, point Bravo, ETA ninety, nine zero, minutes," Killian replied.

"Confirmed, Cobra One-Five. Will provide further intel as situation evolves. Viper Zero-Two-Two out." Jordan dropped her hand away from the throat microphone and slung the waiting pack onto her back. She tugged the tension straps to secure it in place and then collected her rifle bag, placing it over her left shoulder.

Unconsciously, Jordan caressed her ring finger with the tip of her thumb, the absence of the recently placed engagement ring surprisingly noticeable for having only been there three months. She resisted the urge to sigh. Jordan was a professional and professionals don't let these sorts of thoughts interfere with their missions.

Jordan compartmentalized her thoughts as she had been trained, tucking memories of Brian neatly into place so that she would be free of distraction. After making a final check of the small cave, Jordan tossed a small canister from her vest into the middle of floor before she ducked out of the low entrance. The canister's internal timer counted down five seconds before it began to spray a special, acrid-smelling chemical into the air. MI6 operatives the stuff called 'Spook Be Gone'. The fine mist filled the small cave and covered everything it touched in an ammonia based film formulated to destroy DNA evidence as well as kill any scent. Jordan disliked the smell of the chemical but she was long gone when the device triggered.

To be continued in <u>"Awaken"; book one of the Children of Divinity trilogy</u>.

Reaper's Return

The Chronicles of Aesirium, Book One

By Ren Cummins

Chapter One: Rom

Rom leaned close, hugging her friend. "Count to a thousand. If I'm not back by then, run home." Rain pelted the tattered umbrella just loudly enough to mask the chattering of the two girls' teeth; Rom wiped away a clump of her unnaturally white hair from her face so she could look directly into her friend's eyes. Finally, Kari's head bobbed in as much as shiver as a nod. Leaving before either one of them could talk her out of it, Rom pressed the umbrella into Kari's hands and vaulted the fence into the unknown beyond. She didn't like the idea of leaving Kari there, but they needed to move fast if they didn't want to be late, and the rainfall was slowing them down. Plus, Rom reminded herself for the forty-seventh time, there were monsters out here past the fields.

Facing a choice between slow caution and fast defensiveness, Rom chose the latter. The orphanage's standard issue long dress and jacket protected her against the hundred small whips of the thorns and sharp leaves as she first began to make her way through the plants. After only a few moments of it, she grew annoyed with the many slight stings and pushed off from the ground, using her unnatural degree of skill to cover ten, twenty, as much as thirty meters in a leap. She was never able to really push herself like this: the rooms at the orphanage were small, and the tiny courtyard used for their afternoon constitutional was only barely big enough for the children's daily game of "try to hit ratgirl before she gets away". Plus, Rom didn't like to jump as far as she knew she could, if any of the other children were around to make fun of her. Her hair was unique enough; no reason to give them any other excuse to tease. For a few moments like this, it felt like flying. They said that there were animals out in the Wild that could fly too, far from Oldtown-Against-The-Wall, where the sort of thing like being different could get you punished; but flying was said to be a "challenge to the Wall itself", and was a crime listed among the worst of them.

Five hundred meters out, a distant lightning flash lit up the area near the landmark drawn on the map they'd been given – the wrecked remains of one of the large Machines, left partially-submerged in the ground. She'd seen drawings of them in the daily class sessions, and a few of the larger and simpler constructs were still left rusting around the edges of the fields, but this was the first time she'd seen one of the latter generations of them with her own eyes. *They probably looked less unsettling in the daylight*, she told herself. *Or when it wasn't raining. Or both.*

The actual constructs which had been built to tend to the fields had been simple – designed for the functions they required. Thus they were boxy, blatantly mechanical things – but when the constructs began to make their own machines, their designs took on a much more organic look. They had never known why the Machines began building new Machines, much less why they had built them so unrestrained by the tenets of apparent efficiency; but one thing was certain. When the Machines began to create other Machines, they made them look like *people*.

All the historical lessons the matrons had taught her came back to her with that single strike of lightning as she looked upon what could only be described as a face – albeit one which had to be ten meters in height – half-submerged in the dirt and dramatically overgrown with the brush and plant life left unattended and wild this far out beyond the fence line. As her eyes readjusted to the darkness, she could make out the darker shadows of what must be a shoulder, an arm, and so on. The Machine had to have stood more than ten times as tall as she was, she decided. She shivered, but was pretty sure it wasn't from the rain. She wished Kari were there to see it: this was old Science, and there were few things her friend loved more than that.

Her eyes caught a smaller patch of darkness near the face, a slight movement, roughly boy-shaped.

"Cousins?" she yelled. "Is that you?" Rom growled, spitting out a mouthful of rainwater. With the rain crashing down on the metal shell of the ruined Machine, there could be someone yelling right into her face and she probably wouldn't hear it.

She took a half-step closer when there was a great commotion from behind her; it registered only briefly what a wonder it was that she could hear it, but a growing ache in her stomach seemed to be accompanied by a strange enhancement of all her senses, as if time were slowing down. She'd felt this before in the orphanage courtyard; her body seemed to react to certain situations by seeing everything more clearly, more distinctly, making her more aware of everything as it was happening.

And now, in spite of the rain, she could make out three sets of footsteps – one the hurried run of a girl, and the other, two pairs of feet, most definitely not human. Kari's voice rushed at Rom even more quickly than her feet.

"Rom!!! Help!!" her friend screamed, from somewhere still beyond her in the overgrowth.

Rom stood in the center of the clearing, and her eyes looked quickly around her for anything she could use as a defense or a weapon – a rock, a stick, anything – but in the falling rain, all she could see was mud and water, pooling up around and leaking into her tattered boots. Whatever it was out there, Rom hoped it was small enough that she could kick it until it went away.

Cupping her hands to the sides of her mouth, she called to her friend through the darkness. "Over here!"

A moment later, Kari burst through the branches, still clutching the battered umbrella. Right behind her by a scant breath, a large feline creature jumped into the clearing as well. Lightning crashed somewhere far behind the girls, but momentarily coated the clearing in a silvery brightness that gave them both a clear look at what had been chasing Kari. It stood shoulder-to-shoulder with them both, its grey fur matted by the rain, with yellowed horns emerging from just in front of its ears and curling back around to angle slightly outwards past each side of its jaws. Across its back was what looked like a black leather folded shell, extending from just below its neck and down to its long tail. From its belly down, it was coated in mud, and its golden eyes were rimmed in red, and a sickly green foam curled around the corners of its fanged mouth. It reared back at the flash of lightning, but Rom could still see it silhouetted in place when the darkness once more engulfed them all. Though the lightning might have disoriented it, it evidently realized that a second potential prey stood before it, and it paused to adjust for its next attack.

"Get behind me," Rom said. "When I tell you, run to the Machine back there." Her eyes glanced to the umbrella, and, without thinking, took it from Kari's hands. It wasn't much, but it would have to do.

"M-machine?" Kari said, her curiosity threatening to overcome her fear.

"Don't study it; you need to *hide* in it!" Rom hissed. "Please, Kari, just think of this like another game of hide from Milando!" she added, referring to one of the larger bullies also living in the orphanage.

"Hide?" Kari repeated.

"Yes, I need you to wait for me over there while I go box his ears, nothing to worry about."

She could sense, somehow, the creature preparing to make its move. The beast seemed to recognize her confidence and crouched, she thought, preparing to jump at Rom. It was basically predatory, and it saw her as getting in the way of what it wanted to eat.

"Get ready, Kari," she whispered above the sound of the rain. Rom could see, even in the darkness, its back muscles and hind legs shuddering, tensing. The horns would be a problem, she figured, so a strike for the head was out; the ends of the horns would keep her from getting to its throat, and that shell was going to make it impossible to get at from above. It was an impressively made monster; Rom thought that if it wasn't trying right now to kill her, she'd probably think it was brilliant.

She spun the umbrella over in her hand, feeling its balance. The handle might be strong enough to use as a weapon – it was metal with a solid wooden handle, and came to a metal end the length of her hand. Absently, she considered that it was a poor choice to bring out into a lightning storm, but she would hopefully be able to regret that later. *That was one nice thing about regret*, Rom thought, you *can always do it later if you're too busy*.

The creature tensed one last time and pounced. Even before the creature's paws left the ground, Rom was telling Kari to run, even pushing her back with her left hand to make sure she moved. Rom ducked slightly to draw the beast's eyes down and away from her friend, hoping as well to create a smaller target for her much larger opponent.

Time seemed to drag even more – the monster looked like it was jumping almost comically slowly. Rom looked closely; she could somehow perceive the angle of its jump, and knew instinctively that by shifting her weight to the right and rolling down and back across its path, she would avoid its front paws and bring her up in a position to land the first strike. With its weight, claws and teeth as its obvious advantages, she would have to play on its disadvantages – its size and desperation for food meant she might be able to out maneuver it, and hopefully outthink it. The rain, mud and darkness, she hoped, would keep everything else even for them both.

Hopefully.

She dove under the angle of its jump and stabbed upwards as it passed harmlessly past her, feeling a warm streak of its blood spray across her face and arms. It let out a loud cry and hit the ground unsteadily. Instantly, she felt a pang of remorse. It wasn't the beast's fault it was attacking her and Kari. It was just trying to get food, and...

"You've got babies!" Rom breathed. "Oh no."

The animal was between her and Kari, and she could see Kari making her way quickly to the machine's head. But the creature must have decided that Kari would make a less difficult catch. It quickly spun away from Rom and was after Kari in a heartbeat.

"No!" Rom yelled, leaping up after the creature. "Run, Kari!" she screamed.

She landed on the animal's back, just above the shell and behind the horns. She grabbed on to one of the horns with her right hand to both secure herself and to try to somehow steer the cat from her friend. The animal stopped running, and turned its attention on trying to rid itself of this unwanted rider. It leapt backwards in a completely circular flip, Rom somehow managing to keep herself from falling off. It spun its head from side to side, raking the girl's legs with its horns.

But then, with a snarl, it opened what Rom had mistakenly believed to be the shell on its back – and two great leathern wings unfurled. Before Rom could jump free, the cat leapt into the air, and they flew up into the night sky. She dropped the parasol so she could hold onto the horns with both hands, and gripped the cat tightly above the shoulder blades with her legs.

Quests & Answers   213

Higher, higher, they flew, up towards the clouds themselves.

Below her, she could see the distant blue glow of the town's defensive barrier, mirrored by flowing sheets of lightning in the clouds above. She could feel the creature's panic and fear – it wanted to run, but it was conflicted by a need to acquire food for its young. Rom clung to the creature, however, hoping they would soon descend to a low enough altitude that she might safely drop off without injury, but they continued to ascend higher and higher. The rain crashed against her, a sensation washed away by a single thought: *I'm flying*.

The momentary exhilaration lasted only thus; replaced by the realization that it was not so much flying as it was riding; but for a sudden jolt and the ground would break her into small pieces.

She frowned, blinking against the falling rain. "Hang it," she grumbled.

Just as she thought her situation couldn't get any worse, a light – brighter than any she had ever before seen – filled her vision with a thunderclap that stopped her heart and burst her ears.

Distantly, she felt as if she was falling, slowly, insubstantial like a snowflake, drifting down towards the far away ground; helpless on the winter breeze.

To be continued in <u>"Reaper's Return", book one of the Chronicles of Aesirium</u>.

ABOUT THE AUTHORS

H. L. REASBY

H. L. Reasby is a writer and editor who resides in the beautiful (and rainy) Pacific Northwest. She lives there with her beloved husband, two deranged cats, and two crazed dogs. Reading and writing (of course) top the list of personal interests, but H. L. also enjoys movies, gaming (roleplaying games being her favorite), and spending time with friends.

Drawn to literature from an early age, it was amusingly enough the need to fill a course credit in college which started her on the track to writing. Inspired by the Ripley character from the "Alien" movies, H. L. enjoys telling the stories of strong and courageous women, fueled by the dream of creating new heroes built on the foundation of classical mythologies. In addition to her literary creative outlets, she has embraced the new digital age, emphasizing networking and the unfettered elements of publishing that the internet has so graciously provided.

Other books by H. L. Reasby:

Sekhmet's Light Trilogy:

Akhet

Peret

Shomu (Coming Spring 2012)

GARTH REASBY

Garth Reasby has always enjoyed creating and has channeled his creative energies into art, music, prop making, and writing. A renaissance man, Garth has had various jobs ranging from bodyguarding religious figures to project management.

"Awaken" is Garth's first novel and allowed him to borrow concepts and experiences from his rich personal history and form them into a very modern tale of super heroes in the real world. In addition to a follow-up novel in the Children of Divinity series, Garth is preparing works for a number of anthologies and a new fantasy series.

Garth was born and raised in the Pacific Northwest and currently lives there with his wife Heather Reasby, also an author, and their menagerie of animals. When Garth does find time to relax he enjoys reading, comic books, video games, music, camping, and off-roading, as well as putting a few hours in at the range to keep up his firearm skills.

Other books by Garth Reasby:

The Children of Divinity trilogy:

Awaken

Evolve (coming Summer 2012)

QUIANA KIRKLAND

Quiana Kirkland is the Editor-in-Chief of Talaria Press and lives and works in the Seattle area. She became passionate about writing and helping others write while attending Bryn Mawr College, outside of Philadelphia. Quiana has edited various written works for over a decade before coming to Talaria Press. Her goal at Talaria Press is to publish books that inspire, entrance, and fill the reader with the spirit of adventure.

Quiana loves cooking, crafting, and, above all, reading. She would like to say that she lives in a crumbling Gothic mansion, but she does not. She does live in a cozy house with a large, but usually well-behaved pet.

REN CUMMINS

The adventure began around the time a few astronauts were nancing about on the moon. There may have been offroading, there may have been golf; but all he saw was one giant leap for mankind. He was reading comic books and dreaming of when he'd get to grow up to be Spiderman. The tales of heroes, old and new, infected his otherwise somber way of thinking, and what came out on the other side resolved itself into a love of adventure.

One night, not too long ago, as he told his daughter a bedtime story - one they were making up on the spot - it just clicked for him. Her enthusiastic expression and engagement reminded him of the one commonality of all his experiences that had meant so much to him: storytelling. He returned to writing, to telling stories.

Rumors also persist that he may have invented some sort of time machine. But... that's another story for another time.

* * * * *

Born in California, Ren Cummins lived in three more states and one other country before eventually settling down in Seattle, Washington. There with his wife and their daughter, their two dogs and one of the heaviest cats in existence, he juggles a love of writing, music, science fiction and the occasional desire to make an honest buck.

"The Morrow Stone" was nominated for 2010's Steampunk Book of the Year.

Other books by Ren Cummins:

The Chronicles of Aesirium:

Reaper's Return

The Morrow Stone

The City of the Dead

Reaper's Flight

Into the Blink

The Crook and the Blade

The Middle Age: A Geek's Journey from Boy to Man

Volume 1

The Emissary Files

The Old Bones (Coming Fall 2012)

ABOUT TALARIA PRESS:

Publishing by and for the people.

Talaria Press is dedicated to helping authors bring their stories to greater audiences through the use of new media. We at Talaria Press believe that readers should be able to buy the books they want to read, in the format that best suits their lives. We believe that authors should not have to exchange their rights and profits to find an audience. As lovers of books, everyone at Talaria Press strives to help authors shape good manuscripts into great books.

Contrary to fears that technology will eradicate reading, Talara Press believes in the transformative power of technology and is committed to finding innovative ways to connect books to readers.

Visit Talaria Press' virtual headquarters at:

www.talariapress.com

Made in the USA
Charleston, SC
16 March 2012